CANDLELIGHT

Supreme

"EXACTLY WHAT WOULD YOU CALL WHAT HAPPENED BETWEEN US LAST NIGHT?" SHAY DEMANDED STUBBORNLY.

"Last night was most probably something that shouldn't have happened at all," Kurt rasped in a hard voice. "It's not that I'm trying to run away from this . . . chemistry between us, Shay, but I refuse to be railroaded into a situation I'm leery of."

"Railroaded!" burst from Shay's lips. "Just what do you mean by railroaded?"

"I mean that you want to think of last night as the beginning of a future for us, Shay. That's fine . . . for you, but not for me."

Shay shook her head. "You know last night was fantastic . . . and everything that happened between us was fantastic. But you're so afraid of committing even a small part of yourself to a woman, that you'll deny us both a chance at happiness." She paused, glaring at him. "You're a flaming coward, Kurt Barron!"

CANDLELIGHT SUPREMES

QUANTITY SALES

INDIVIDUAL SALES

BREATHLESS
TEMPTATION

Eleanor Woods

A CANDLELIGHT SUPREME

Published by
Dell Publishing Co., Inc.
1 Dag Hammarskjold Plaza
New York, New York 10017

Dell ® TM 681510, Dell Publishing Co., Inc.

Candlelight Supreme is a trademark
of Dell Publishing Co., Inc.

Candlelight Ecstasy Romance®, 1,203,540, is a registered trademark of Dell Publishing Co., Inc., New York, New York.

ISBN: 0-440-10837-3

Printed in the United States of America

January 1987

10 9 8 7 6 5 4 3 2 1

WFH

To Our Readers:

We are pleased and excited by your overwhelmingly positive response to our Candlelight Supremes. Unlike all the other series, the Supremes are filled with more passion, adventure, and intrigue, and are obviously the stories you like best.

In months to come we will continue to publish books by many of your favorite authors as well as the very finest work from new authors of romantic fiction. As always, we are striving to present unique, absorbing love stories —the very best love has to offer.

Breathtaking and unforgettable, Supremes follow in the great romantic tradition you've come to expect *only* from Candlelight Romances.

Your suggestions and comments are always welcome. Please let us hear from you.

Sincerely,

The Editors
Candlelight Romances
1 Dag Hammarskjold Plaza
New York, New York 10017

CHAPTER ONE

"Oh, Kurt. You have no idea how I've missed you," the sultry voice murmured invitingly. "Don't you think you've been terribly unfair to me? We haven't managed to spend a single second alone in weeks."

The rustle of clothing caused Shay Michaels, who was kneeling in the midst of the miniature jungle of greenery, quickly to place her watering can on the floor and part the leaves of a tall, full corn plant and stare at the two people standing a mere arm's length from her.

The woman, a curvaceous individual, her blond hair swirled into fashionable disarray, was resting her hands on a gorgeously wide pair of shoulders, her scarlet-tipped fingers caressing that same width and firmness while the tall, powerfully built dark-haired man stood totally indifferent—his hands casually resting on the blonde's waist.

Shay, her blue eyes brimming with amusement, changed to a more comfortable position on her faded denim-clad knees and craned her neck in order not to miss a single gesture by the pair. Oh, this was great, she thought excitedly as she watched Kurt's reaction to such an obvious line. It mattered little to Shay that she was in Kurt's office, because this was almost as good as when she was eleven and had hidden in the hedgerow, watching him kiss Louise McKinley. The Colonel, the uncle who had raised Kurt, had been away at the time, and Kurt had taken full advantage of his absence to perfect his craft of seduction. If only she hadn't giggled, Shay remembered, Kurt would never have known she was there. But she had, and he did, and all hell broke loose. Afterward he'd ignored her for weeks. It had been a miserable time for her.

Still, she supposed that what she was doing now *could* be considered eavesdropping.

Oh, well, she couldn't let a little thing like that worry her. Watching Kurt was an education in itself. Even if she had been doing it practically all her life, it was still fascinating. And now, she was getting to see yet another aspect of the great Barron in action, and nothing short of dynamite was going to move her from her vantage point. Since taking on the care and rotation of the greenery for Barron Industries, Shay had found it to be the most "entertaining" of all her plant rental clients.

"Your husband is a friend and business associate of mine, Tessa," Kurt replied with an underlying thread of impatience in his deep, raspy voice. He stepped back, his hands dropping to his sides, but Tessa followed like a magnet toward a piece of steel.

There was an expression in the rough features of Kurt's face that reminded Shay of disgust . . . at least that's what it looked like to her. And she knew for certain, when she saw that tiny muscle in his cheek beginning to pulse, that he was annoyed.

She'd seen that same pulsation when she was ten and had smeared paint on the driver's side of his car. He'd caught her and hauled her across his knee. Shay remembered calling him a bastard while his large hand was applying punishment to her rear. She also remembered how confused she'd been by his mocking response that he sure as hell was one. When she'd looked up the word later, she'd been terribly embarrassed. She'd only repeated what she'd heard his uncle say. The old man was cruelly blunt, and loud to boot, and Shay had heard him telling her mother about the "shameful" way his neice—Kurt's mother—had deserted her son.

Shay inspected Kurt's face further, seeing what she considered a very positive sign of impatience or anger or probably both, as the warmth left his stormy black eyes and they became cold as ice. She knew each line, each

9

tiny scar—there were two—as well as she knew her own. She knew the shape of his nose was "the Barron gift," as the Colonel used to repeat, and Shay also knew that Kurt hated it.

"Former husband, Kurt," Tessa purred, running one hand over his dark hair that almost—but didn't quite—brush the collar of his immaculate white shirt, her fingers curving possessively to the shape of his neck. "John and I are divorced now. He shouldn't care at all who I go out with."

"You have your standards, Tessa, and I have mine," Kurt said firmly. Shay watched the tightening of his facial muscles that accentuated the stubborn slant of his jawline. This time she could see that he was more direct in his attempt to escape the clutches of Tessa Graham. He grasped her wrists and firmly removed her hands. Shay grinned. Didn't the silly woman know by now that Kurt didn't like to be fondled by a woman . . . unless he initiated the action?

"I'm having a few people in tomorrow evening," Tessa countered without missing a beat, oblivious to the fact that the man facing her was staring at her without an ounce of affection in his gaze. "I hope you'll join us."

Shay could hardly believe her ears. Couldn't Tessa see that Kurt wanted nothing to do with her? Where on earth was her pride?

"I'll keep that in mind," Kurt answered

without promise. "Now if you'll excuse me, Tessa, I have people waiting to see me." He moved purposefully toward the door, opened it, and waited for his guest to depart. Tessa did so, but as she drew even with Kurt, she let her fingers trail provocatively across his chest. It was all Shay could do to keep from giggling at the murderous glint that sprang to life in Kurt's eyes.

He closed the door with an explosive "Damn!," then turned and walked determinedly toward the bank of greenery where Shay was kneeling. He came to a halt in almost the exact same spot where he'd been standing when Tessa was trying to seduce him. In an unexpected move Kurt leaned down, his large hands braced against his widespread knees, and peered at the unrepentant eavesdropper.

"Enjoying yourself . . . again?" he asked mockingly.

Shay shrugged, adopting an air of indifference despite the veiled threat she saw lurking in the depths of his eyes.

"Can I help it if women insist on trailing you like bloodhounds and accost you at every turn?" she asked facetiously.

"No, I suppose you can't," Kurt said harshly. "But you sure as hell could make your presence known."

"If I did that, then I wouldn't get such fascinating tidbits for the book I might decide to

11

write one day on the loves of Kurt Barron. I should think you'd like the idea of seeing your life story in print. On the other hand, I do wish you would add something a little spicier to your routine, Kurt. From what I've seen in the past couple of months, you could use some new material."

"Really?" Kurt murmured icily. "And just exactly what is it that you've 'seen'?"

"Well, for one thing," she began, "When Tessa Graham was trying to put the make on you, you were backtracking like a crayfish. That's bad for your image. 'Kurt daawling, I've missed you so,'" she mimicked, and grinned. "For a moment there I thought I was about to see, firsthand, the great Barron in another of his sizzling love scenes. Unfortunately, you got cold feet. You reversed so promptly, you almost landed in the schefflera."

"Cold feet have nothing to do with it." He scowled. "Her ex-husband happens to be a friend of mine."

"It's nice to know you have scruples. I always thought there was more of the Colonel in you than you cared to admit," Shay replied matter-of-factly. "I'm sure to some men, friendship with Tessa's husband could be neatly overlooked."

"How kind of you to place your stamp of approval on my actions," Kurt snapped. "Now get your behind out from your hiding place, before I drag you out."

"Tsk, tsk. And to think you were so polite and gentle with dear, sweet Tessa," she was muttering as she worked her way through the wall of greenery that banked a glass wall on one entire side of Kurt's spacious office. "Unfortunately, I have the 'pleasure' of knowing the real Kurt Barron, who at certain times can be a real jerk."

As soon as her brown, curly head was clear, Kurt reached down and caught her upper arms and brought her to her feet, his not-too-careful grasp causing the bottom edge of her sweatshirt to bunch up beneath her arms.

Shay glared at him as she corrected the mishap, but not before Kurt saw the honey-colored skin of her midriff tanned by the Arizona sun, and a scar left there from when she was nine years old and couldn't get down from the tree she'd climbed.

A curious blend of emotions stirred within Kurt as old memories floated past. Having lived next door to the Michaels, he'd rescued Shay that day, as he'd done on previous occasions and continued to do till he left the Colonel's house to go and make his fortune. Shay Michaels and her mischief-making ways had become woven in his life like a long, untidy string one was unable to break. After the Colonel's death, when Kurt found himself the old

13

man's heir, he'd returned to Flagstaff and the house where he'd been raised. He'd also settled somewhat into the same routine with Shay.

"What do you mean, a jerk? What is that supposed to mean?" he asked shortly. He caught hold of her elbow and half pushed, half led her through to another room that was decorated and furnished much the same as a small den. Shay had been in the room a few times before and knew that it also contained a well-stocked fridge, and a closet with several changes of clothes for Kurt. A complete bath made it a smaller version of home away from home.

While Kurt was busy at the bar, she eyed the two long sofas, wondering if they were Hideabeds. She'd never had the courage to ask. It was a silly idea anyway. What on earth would he want with two beds? She felt positive either of the sofas—surely they were sofas—were adequate for some of the more intimate moments that cropped up during his office hours. All in all it was a very cozy arrangement, she decided.

"You didn't answer my question."

"I'm thinking about it," and a million other things as well, she thought without hesitating. "Actually, you've always struck me as being on your best behavior with other women. Yet with me, you act like a sore-tailed cat."

"My most humble apologies, Miss Michaels."
He grinned mockingly. "I'll make a point to do
better in the future. Okay?"

"I suppose so."

"What's on your mind now?" he asked resignedly as he walked over and handed her a
frosty canned soda, catching sight of the frown
settling over her attractive features.

"For one thing," Shay said spiritedly, looking
pointedly from "his" choice of beverage for
her to his own Scotch and water, "I'm old
enough to have an alcoholic drink if I want one.
You don't have to watch after me anymore like
an overbearing brother. Or has that fact es-
caped you?"

Kurt watched curiously but with a touch of
cynical indulgence as she flopped down onto
the sofa. Though her body was small and slim,
she was as graceful as a gazelle. Funny, he
thought rather surprisedly, Shay the tomboy
seemed to have grown into a very attractive
young woman right under his very nose. "I'm
noticing," he said roughly, his gaze touching on
the thrust of her breasts beneath the shapeless
sweatshirt, then shifting to her face and the
blue-velvet darkness of her eyes. He sat down
beside her. "Would you care for a glass of wine
instead? Perhaps a beer?"

"No, thanks."

"Then why the fuss?" He frowned. He did a
quick bit of mental arithmetic and was amazed

to discover that "little" Shay Michaels, who had followed him around like a devoted but obnoxious puppy for years, was now a twenty-three-year-old woman.

"Because I resent you still treating me as if I'm ten years old, Kurt. I'm a grown woman, for Pete's sake."

"So you are," he replied in such a vague manner—or so it seemed to Shay—that she was ready to box his ears. "How's Flagstaff's finest plant rental service doing?" Not only had she grown up, Kurt told himself, but beneath those baggy old shirts she insisted on wearing, he'd seen a beautiful, slim body.

"Growing," Shay replied, and it was. The plant rental service and the floral shop she'd started on a shoestring were indeed growing beyond her wildest expectations. No, it wasn't her business that was responsible for her bad mood, but there was nothing to be gained by pointing this out. To the man seated beside her, she would always be the aggravating brat next door. She dismissed the issue from her mind. There were far more important things to think about. Such as how to make sure Kurt Barron would never again dismiss her as a mere child. A mischievous smile stole over her face as she wondered at his reaction if he were to see her in the dress she'd worn last night when she'd gone out dancing with Roger.

She closed her eyes and let her head drop

back against the muted shades of rust-and-brown-striped fabric and propped the heels of her tennis shoes on the edge of the mahogany table sitting between the two sofas. She had a pretty good idea dear old Kurt would quite likely suffer a coronary, considering just about everything about her life-style drew criticism from him.

"When was the last time you saw Jane?"

"Over a week ago," Shay replied tonelessly, without opening her eyes or making the slightest change in her position. Damn it! she silently seethed. She resented being looked upon by Kurt as some sort of comfortable fixture in his life. Well, then, a tiny voice asked, exactly what is it you want from him? Do you want him to be your lover?

Heaven's no! she all but answered out loud. The thought was so ridiculous it brought a rush of color to her cheeks.

"How *is* Jane?" Kurt asked again in an annoyed voice. "And what the hell's the matter with you?" he demanded. "You act like you're in a daze."

"She's fine," Shay snapped, unable to understand her own puzzling thoughts, and resenting the confusion surrounding them. "Her husband is fine and so is her daughter. Care to try the weather next? I didn't hear the forecast for the day, but I'll be happy to dial the local number that gives out such information and relay it to you."

She plunked the canned drink down on the table without having even tasted it, and sprang to her feet, suddenly overwhelmed by a sense of confusion. "I have to go, Kurt. Thanks for the drink, I'll see you later," she threw over her shoulder as she hurried toward the door.

"Wait a minute, kid," Kurt yelled as the door slammed behind her. Damnation! he silently cursed. He ran a wide hand over his square chin as he stared thoughtfully at the door.

Something was bothering Shay and he wanted to know what it was. He'd call Jane Corley later and see if she had any idea what was bothering her younger sister. Kurt felt a certain protectiveness toward Shay and her sister Jane. Though Jane was married and had a three-year-old daughter, Shay had been more or less on her own since their mother's death three years ago.

He walked over to the massive walnut desk where he'd been working when interrupted by Tessa's arrival. Funny, he mused as he sat down in the chair and leaned back, he'd once been engaged to Jane Michaels Corley. She'd come to him practically in tears, asking him to help her. Her widowed mother had been pushing her to marry a certain young man from a wealthy family, and Jane knew the only way to throw a crimp into her mother's plans was to come up with an equally wealthy suitor. Kurt had fit the bill perfectly. He'd always been like a brother, Jane told him, and she knew she could count on him. Knowing Suzanne Michaels and her cold, calculating plans for both her daughters, Kurt hadn't hesitated in becoming "engaged" to Jane. It was during that time that she met Ted Corley, a dental student. A week after his graduation they were married. Suzanne had been livid. With Jane's defection from the ranks Suzanne dedicated herself to seeing that Shay didn't make the same mistake.

A mocking grin of amusement spread over his face as he remembered the dilemma Suzanne Michaels had found herself in when she'd learned Kurt was to become her son-in-law. He'd vastly enjoyed watching the struggle in her eyes as she'd silently weighed the illegitimacy of his birth against the remarkable fortune he'd amassed. It had taken only minutes for her to decide—as Kurt had known it would —thus giving Jane a much-needed breather. He'd always considered Suzanne a hard, cold person, and after that particular episode he was certain of it. She reminded him in some ways of his own mother. They'd both been selfish women, but at least Suzanne had kept her children with her.

Kurt's expression hardened as he remembered the hurt and frustration he had felt at being dumped on the Colonel. He'd felt betrayed when news came that his mother, whom he had never really known all that well, had been killed in a plane crash. In his childish way of looking at life then, he had hated her for leaving him.

Knowing he was illegitimate was something Kurt had been forced to deal with at an early age. His eyes narrowed against the pain and humiliation he'd felt as a child when his uncle would discuss Kurt's mother's mistake openly in the child's presence, being ever so brutal with his assessment of his niece. Yet as Kurt grew older, he began to see that the old man's sharp tongue was a far cry from the sense of fair play that dwelled in his heart. Nor was the Colonel ashamed of his nephew. He took Kurt everywhere with him, and treated him like an adult. There was no affection in the relationship, and as Kurt matured, he became almost as cynical and brutal in his thoughts as his uncle.

Nicholas Pappolas stood tall and erect at the window that overlooked the section of the grounds that ended at the edge of the stream meandering through his property. He was a big man, with iron-gray hair and blue eyes. At the moment he was miserable, his mood as colorless as the grass left brown by the biting cold of the first freeze.

In short, he told himself bluntly, he was

lonely. He turned his head, casting a critical eye over the room behind him. It was perfect . . . as it should have been. It had cost him a small fortune. When the decorator finished, Nicholas had been pleased. Now it seemed to shriek out at him with its unearthly silence. For some reason it reminded him of a tomb.

He sighed as he turned back to the window and his lonely assessment of nothing in particular. There should be some gentle clutter about the room and the grounds—just as there should be the sound of grandchildren laughing and crying and giggling. His dark eyes took on a faraway look as memories drifted in. Of all the regrets in his life it was not having a family of his own that hurt him most.

Oh, he had sisters and brothers and the usual number of nieces and nephews that ran in large families. But since his recent illness and subsequent back surgery, he'd had time on his hands, time in which really to take a long, hard look at his life. What he'd seen hadn't pleased him.

In his mind's eye he saw the face of his lovely Emily—heard her laughter, and wondered—as he had so often done in the past, especially in the past few weeks—what had become of her. He wondered about the baby and if it lived. For there had been a baby, he knew in his heart, even if Emily had disappeared before confirming his suspicions. Too many factors

21

pointed to it being so. There'd been the sudden thickening about her waist, and—his heart told him so. He'd known her body as well as he knew his own. And during the last dinner they'd shared, she'd hardly touched her food. Afterward, she'd been so overcome by nausea she'd had to leave the table.

They'd met on a warm summer's day in San Francisco. At first she'd been determined to keep her distance, pointedly ignoring Nicholas's attempts to get to know her. Finally out of desperation, he'd gotten the manager of the hotel to speak to the beautiful dark-haired woman, reassuring her that Mr. Pappolas was single and respectable.

Nicholas smiled as he remembered almost every word, every event that happened during the remainder of that weekend and all the others to follow. He thought back to the tragic story he'd heard and how his heart had gone out to his beloved Emily.

Her husband had been in a terrible automobile accident a few months prior to her meeting Nicholas, leaving him bedridden for life. His mind had been impaired, and it was very seldom that he even recognized Emily. Her brief vacation to San Francisco came about at the urging of her best friend, who promised to baby-sit Emily's husband.

When he'd learned that Emily was married, Nicholas's instincts told him to leave her alone.

But by the end of that first weekend he was completely taken with the haunting look he saw in her eyes and the gentle air about her. He found himself head over heels in love for the first time, and was shocked to discover the hatred he felt for the husband keeping them apart. For the next six months the one weekend a month they shared became the highlight of Nicholas's life.

His gaze narrowed as he continued to remember. If only he hadn't demanded that she leave her husband and go away with him. He could still see the glimmer of panic that sprang to her eyes at his urging. It had been their worst quarrel, Nicholas telling her that he wanted her to have his baby. She disappeared later that evening, and Nicholas never saw her again. But, he reflected, defending his actions of twenty odd years ago, the thought of her carrying his child had excited him beyond all bounds of common sense. After his anger toward her for having run away from him cooled down, he'd hired detectives to look for Emily; but it was as if she had disappeared from the face of the earth.

She'd never actually told him the name of the small Nevada town where she lived, but Nicholas had gotten a peek at her driver's license. The fact that he had that information had given him a false sense of security. By the time the detective got around to checking out the address given him by Nicholas, he learned Emily's husband had died, and that the pregnant Emily and her three-year-old daughter had left the area. There was no forwarding address . . . no information to be gotten from neighbors . . . and Nicholas had been devastated. He'd also been shocked to learn she and her husband had had a child. He felt betrayed that Emily hadn't shared that part of her life with him.

With an angry sigh at himself for having let the past slip into his thoughts and defeat him yet again, he left his place by the window and went back to his large chair by the fireplace. As he made himself comfortable, he thought again of how he'd been forced to accept that Emily hadn't wanted to be found. In the end he had had to abide by her unspoken wishes. A few months later he met and married Elena. And though he hadn't loved his wife and had definitely married her on the rebound, Nicholas quietly mused, he'd been very fond of her. The fact that she couldn't have children, though, had come as a blow to them both. He'd built the shipping line that bore his name into a worldwide corporation and he was a wealthy man. He hid from Elena his disappointment that he would never have a son to carry on his name, and they'd had a happy life together till her death five years ago.

Now an idea that had been teasing him for

several months began to taunt him again. He wanted to find Emily, and the son he knew in his very soul she'd given him. This time, no matter what the initial report indicated, he wouldn't give up. She was out there somewhere, waiting for him. He had only to find her.

He got up and walked over to a large desk in one corner of the room and opened a drawer. It was time to move, he told himself; he'd put off making a definite decision far too long. A single, folded page from a newspaper was removed from the drawer and opened, his long, capable fingers rubbing at the crease. In the lower right-hand corner a heavily outlined square had been boldly circled in red. Nicholas stared at the simply worded ad for several seconds.

He already considered that if he were to find Emily and his child, he could very well stir up quite a scandal if he wasn't careful. There was also the possibility she might not even want to acknowledge their brief affair. Most probably she would have remarried. Nicholas inhaled deeply as he recounted all the "probables" that could just as easily go against him. Then, before he could change his mind, he picked up the receiver and began dialing. If he could have Emily, that would be wonderful. But it was his deep desire to see and get to know his child that more than anything else convinced him to put his plan into action.

At that moment the door opened and Phillip Norcross walked in. His dark eyes showed surprise at finding his uncle at the desk Nicholas used when he had work to do at home.

"Itching to get back at the controls, Uncle Nicholas?" he said pleasantly. Phillip was considerably shorter than Nicholas, but he favored the older man, having the same straight, prominent nose and broad forehead. Where Nicholas's hair was now an attractive gray, Phillip's was still deep black.

At the moment, however, how closely he resembled his uncle was the farthest thing from Phillip's mind. He was annoyed.

Though one of several nephews, he liked to believe he was Nicholas's favorite. When Nicholas had been hospitalized several weeks ago and required back surgery, Phillip had jumped at the chance to be in command of the company. His ego had swollen to an unbelievable size, and he was already envisioning what it all would mean when Nicholas died and he, Phillip, would be head of Pappolas Shipping. He would be in control then, as he should be.

"Hello, Phillip," Nicholas replied. "I'm just tak— Hello," he broke off his conversation with his nephew. "This is Nicholas Pappolas. I'd like to speak with Ian Deaton, please."

Phillip walked over to the desk, curious as to what it was Nicholas was calling about.

"I see," he heard his uncle respond. He then left his number and asked that Ian Deaton call him as soon as possible.

"Trouble?" Phillip asked when the receiver was replaced, his curiosity getting the best of him.

"Not in the usual sense." Nicholas smiled. He leaned forward, his large fists braced against the surface of the desk, feeling an enormous sense of relief that he'd finally gotten started on something that had been bothering him for years. "I need a good detective, and this Ian Deaton has been recommended to me by several of my friends. I'm told he can find anybody almost anywhere in the world."

Phillip frowned. "I wasn't aware we were looking for anyone, Uncle Nicholas. If you'll fill me in on the details, I'll see that it's taken care of without your having to be bothered."

"That's considerate of you, Phillip," Nicholas acknowledged with a nod, "but this is a personal matter." He regarded his nephew enigmatically. What was there about the younger man that aroused his distrust? Nicholas wondered.

"Very well," Phillip said stiffly. "I'll be returning to New York this evening. Are there any messages you want me to take back with me?"

"None that I can think of," Nicholas said smoothly. "I've already spoken with Kathryn. She knows I'll be returning on Tuesday."

"It'll be good having you back," Phillip replied.

Nicholas's gaze narrowed. It wasn't uncommon for Phillip—or any other young man, for that matter—to resent having to give up a brief reign of control of one of the largest shipping giants in the world. But Nicholas felt not only his nephew's resentment, but ripples of hatred emanating from him.

It was time for him to get back to work, Nicholas thought to himself. Phillip was assuming too much and it was going to be a sticky situation for the younger man to take a position of lesser authority.

After a few more moments of tense conversation Phillip said good-bye, anxious to be on his way. As soon as he closed the door, he took a small leather note pad from an inside jacket pocket and quickly wrote down the telephone number of the detective agency Nicholas had called.

Later that evening, after he'd returned to his apartment in New York, Phillip made a telephone call. When the party he was calling answered, he went straight to the point.

"Are you one hundred percent positive that no one else knows Uncle Nicholas has a child?"

"What's the matter?" he was asked. "Losing your nerve?"

"I'll lose a lot more than my nerve if my uncle ever finds out that I have information you gave me verifying that he has a 'love' child."

"You have copies of all the information at my disposal. If that doesn't satisfy you, then perhaps you should hire a detective to verify the story," the party snapped.

Phillip started to say he'd done that very thing, but something stopped him. "Even you wouldn't be stupid enough to try and pull off something this big without evidence backing up your claim."

"How kind of you to say so," the voice replied sarcastically. "By the way, I've been doing some thinking. The amount of money we agreed on isn't enough."

"It's all you're getting."

"Oh, really? Have you considered what would happen if your Uncle Nicholas were to be made privy to the same information you have regarding his child? How would your uncle take it if he were to be 'tipped off' that his honorable nephew was involved in a plot to keep the information from him?"

Phillip's hand clenched into a fist at his side as he listened to the threats. At the moment there was very little he could do, but there was an idea beginning to grow in his mind that he was positive would *eliminate* his most pressing problem. "How much more do you want?"

CHAPTER TWO

Shay stared intently into first one side mirror and then the other as she backed the tan van down the driveway, and to the large greenhouse sitting some distance behind the house where she lived.

"Turn it to the right just a tad," Jane—who was lending a hand with the unloading and offering directions as well—yelled. "Not that much," she cried out. "Turn to the left . . . the left, you idiot! You've just run over the Colonel's favorite rosebush. What on earth will Kurt think?"

"To hell with the Colonel's rosebush and Kurt," Shay yelled right back, never taking her eyes off the mirrors. "I'd like to see that old windbag back this damn van down a half-mile driveway."

"Must you always be defaming my relatives?" a deep male voice called out from over the hedgerow.

Shay let her eyes dart toward the sound for a

second, and encountered Kurt Barron's devilish grin. He was a good head and shoulders taller than the hedge.

"Your relatives, the only two I was ever privileged to meet, left a hell of a lot to be desired, Mr. Barron," she snapped, then returned to the arduous task at hand. "Would you mind telling my sister to move before she goes the same way as your uncle's roses?"

Shay kept her foot on the brake, watching in the mirror as Kurt walked back to where Jane was waving her arms like a windmill. She saw him remove the jacket of the dark, expensive suit he was wearing and lay it across the hedge. The material of his shirt was smooth against the width and depth of his shoulders and chest, flattering his build. His tall body leaned slightly forward as he spoke with Jane. Suddenly both of them laughed, and Shay gripped the steering wheel with annoyance.

She wondered why it had to be that Kurt—with all the locations available to him—had chosen to come back to Flagstaff, to the very same house where he'd lived with his uncle. Worse still, why had her mother seen fit many years ago to buy the smaller property from the Colonel? It annoyed Shay. She would much rather Kurt had chosen someplace else to live.

Her foot eased from the brake to the gas pedal and the van began moving backward. Surely memories of living with the Colonel weren't so wonderful as to make him want to return, she thought sourly. The old man had been abrupt to the point of cruelty. On the other hand—she quietly shrugged—he had taken Kurt in as a baby, and seemed, in his caustic way, to have loved him. At any rate, he'd made Kurt his heir. So in a way the huge, rambling house next door probably seemed like home—which, she admitted ruefully, it was.

"Dammit, Shay! Watch where you're going."

Shay slammed on the brakes and thrust her head out the window in time to see her neighbor rubbing his derrière with one hand and jerking Jane aside with the other.

"Well, if you hadn't been running your mouth ninety miles an hour, you'd have seen me coming," she replied in kind, positively mortified at having been caught daydreaming by the person she was daydreaming about. It had been three days since she'd acted like a two-year-old in his office, and now she was acting like an irresponsible child again.

After finally getting the van as close to the door of the greenhouse as possible, she cut the engine and got out, refusing to even look in the direction of Jane and Kurt. Shay unlocked the door and stalked inside, going immediately to the automatic sprinkler and turning it off. As she turned around, she saw that Kurt had opened the van and was already unloading the plants.

"Where do you want this?" he asked, his face practically hidden by a huge red-margined dracaena. Jane was close behind him with a much smaller weeping fig.

"Over there in that small room." She pointed to the isolation area where she kept all plants for two weeks upon their return to the greenhouse. After that period was over they could be put back with her regular stock. "But you really don't have to do this, you know," she fretted as she practically trotted along behind to open the door for him.

"Oh, really?" Kurt raised a dark brow mockingly. "Would you like for me to dump this damned heavy thing right here and watch you lift it?"

"Must you be so crude?" she asked scathingly, ignoring the giggle from Jane, who was enjoying the fireworks.

"Crude? Me?" Kurt smiled sarcastically. "I'm merely following suit. You've cursed like a sailor ever since I've known you."

"That's a lie and you know it," she replied frostily. One look, however, at her sister's face, and Shay knew she'd lost the battle. She turned on her heel and headed back to the truck, their laughter following her.

Had she turned around and seen it, Shay would have been stunned by the look in Kurt's eyes as he watched the sun catch the coppery highlights of her dark-brown hair, and the way the yellow T-shirt clung to the rounded curve of her breasts, and the sexy length of her tanned legs set off to perfect advantage by the white shorts. Kurt kept on walking beside Jane. He even answered her, several times—didn't he? The only thing he was positive of was an inexplicable explosion going off in his brain. Once the dust had settled, all he could do was stare at Shay, as if he'd never seen her before.

During the time it took for the three of them to unload the van, Shay's and Kurt's caustic remarks aimed at each other had become tempered, mainly through the efforts of Jane, who observed their relationship with a pleased twinkle in her blue eyes.

"Why do I always get invited over on the days you're loading or unloading plants?" Jane asked. They'd finished and she and Kurt were sitting on a couple of wooden crates while Shay misted the plants.

"Because you are a nice person, and I need an extra pair of hands," she was told. Jane groaned and Kurt chuckled. He'd also been roped into the job of helping Shay on numerous occasions, as had a couple of other friends.

"Did Margetta Boyd call you about doing the flowers for the banquet on the twenty-third?"

"Yes. And thanks. That will round out the month nicely for me. If business continues the way it is now, I can plan my trip much sooner than I first thought."

"What trip?" Kurt frowned. Where the hell was she planning on going? he wondered. He hadn't heard anything about a trip.

"To Europe." Shay looked at him over her shoulder. "Surely you remember hearing me talk about it this past year." From the look on his face, however, she knew her babbling on about seeing Europe on her own and at her own pace hadn't penetrated his brain at all. Shay gritted her teeth in frustration. What the hell did she have to do to get Kurt Barron to notice her? Ride naked down Main Street?

"Europe?" Kurt repeated? "Oh . . . yeah. I suppose I do remember hearing you say something about it. When do you plan on leaving?"

"Not for a while yet," she answered dryly. "Unlike you, some of us aren't financially solvent. I still have several months of saving before I take the plunge. Even then, there'll still be the problem of finding someone to look after my business while I'm away."

Kurt muttered something that seemed to convey a degree of sympathy on the surface, but caused Shay to dart a suspicious look at him. "When will your pretty roommate Becky be getting back?" he casually drawled.

"In a day or so. Why? Do you plan on taking her with you to one of Tessa's parties?"

"Just making conversation, Shay." He chuckled. "On the other hand"—he winked at Jane then turned back to Shay—"you might want to see if you can talk Becky into going with me to Aunt Agatha's."

"Oh, Lord!" Shay moaned. She plunked the spray bottle down and wiped her hands on a paper towel she'd stuffed in her pants pocket earlier. Suddenly there was a gleam in her blue eyes. She smiled sweetly at Jane. "If I promise to baby-sit my adorable niece, as well as cook your charming husband a delicious dinner, would you consider going in my place to visit dear, sweet Aunt Agatha?"

"No!"

"Can't we even discuss it?"

"No." Jane shook her head, her shoulder-length black hair gently brushing against her cheek.

"That's a terrible way to be."

"Precisely. And Agatha is a terrible old woman," Jane said sternly. "Besides, she hasn't forgiven me for breaking off my engagement to Kurt."

"But that was years ago," Shay exclaimed, "and she didn't approve of you as a wife for him in the first place. Why would she care who broke it off as long as it was off?"

"I haven't the faintest idea." Jane shrugged, amusement brimming in her brown eyes. "Ask the supposedly injured party," she quipped, waving a slim hand toward a grinning Kurt.

"Well?" Shay demanded.

"She loves me," he comically replied. "Er . . . Aunt Agatha, that is. The circumstances surrounding my birth have made her my personal protector," he added piously, causing even the annoyed Shay to laugh. "Seriously, she is and always has been fond of me. And while she doesn't hate Jane, she still refers to her as that Michaels girl who let me down."

"Well, even though I like her, sort of," Shay hastily added, "why do you insist on dragging me over to see her when you know how she feels about Jane? Doesn't she remember that I'm also a Michaels? Has she forgotten that Jane and I are sisters?"

"Certainly not." Kurt pretended to be shocked. "How dare you suggest that Aunt Agatha's faculties are failing her? For your information, Miss Michaels, she considers you the perfect 'woman' for me."

Both Jane and Shay stared at him with their mouths open.

"Please." He laughed. He reached out and tapped each of them under the chin. "You look like two fish."

"Her mind has completely snapped," Shay managed in a croaking voice.

"She thinks you have spirit." Kurt tried to keep a straight face. "I've tried on numerous occasions to point out that you're just plain rude, but she refuses to see the difference."

"Aunt Agatha is a very discerning lady."

"She's also a very overbearing witch," Jane said sweetly.

"As much as I'm enjoying your company, ladies, and the lavish compliments you're heaping upon the head of my elderly relative, I'm afraid I have to go," Kurt suddenly announced. He dropped a friendly peck on Jane's cheek and promised to come to dinner soon. When he turned to the waiting and suddenly very shy Shay, his expression was guarded. "It would please me if you would go with me to Aunt Agatha's tomorrow evening, honey." His enigmatic gaze went over each feature of her face with such intense searching, Shay began to fidget. "She really does enjoy your company." A devilish grin touched the sensuous curve of his lips. "There's no accounting for taste, is there?"

"Exactly what I was thinking." Shay exhaled deeply, knowing defeat when she saw it. "What time?" she asked resignedly. Agatha Barron had begun the habit of asking Shay to accompany Kurt to dinner at Agatha's house almost a year ago, and for the life of her, Shay couldn't figure out why.

"I'll pick you up at five-thirty."

"Five-thirty? Why so early?"

"Aunt Agatha eats early. Remember?"

"Of course." She shuddered and turned away. "And we mustn't disappoint Aunt Agatha, must we?" She stalked off down an alley of

39

greenery toward the potting section, leaving Jane with Kurt. If Agatha weren't as old as Moses, Shay told herself, she wouldn't bother. But she and the older woman had always gotten along well, and she didn't want to disappoint her. As to what Kurt thought of being saddled with his neighbor every so often for dinner at his aunt's, Shay couldn't say.

Don't be ridiculous, her conscience mocked. There's nothing to say. He still treats you like you were a child. Having you go with him to Agatha's is nothing out of the ordinary—you've always followed him around.

Such a blunt and humiliating thought brought a frown to Shay's face. She began dumping handfuls of black potting soil into containers, muttering all the while about the overbearing people of the world.

Suddenly a warm hand clasped the pivotal point of her shoulder. Shay gave a start, dropping soil onto the counter. "Something bothering you, honey?" Kurt asked huskily from directly behind her. He was so close, in fact, she could feel the nearness of his large body reaching out to her. And she would have recognized the cologne he wore anywhere in the world.

Shay didn't dare turn around. She felt as if every breath in her body were locked permanently in her lungs and that every ounce of blood she possessed had rushed to her brain. She was dizzy and she couldn't breathe. In another moment she was positive she would crumple in a heap at Kurt's feet.

"Shay?" he persisted, a trace of urgency in his voice. Both his hands found their way to her upper arms and turned her facing him. "What's wrong?" he demanded in a raspy whisper. "You've been acting strange lately. Are you having some kind of trouble with a man?" He knew most of the men she was seeing and wondered which one was giving her problems.

At first Shay was tempted to laugh as the faces of the different men she dated rolled through her mind. There was the eternal optimist Wes Pollock, who was unable to understand why she wouldn't go to bed with him; but Shay could handle him. Then there was Bob Ferguson, nice, easygoing Bob. Loads of fun and a confirmed bachelor. Max Wingate and Roger Denison also came to mind. But no, she thought wildly, her gaze locked with Kurt's, none of the aforementioned presented a problem. However . . .

"There is one man," she said softly, managing a slightly martyred expression and deliberately ignoring the concern she saw in his eyes.

"And?" Kurt's fingers digging into her skin made her wince. Did she have a lover? Again he thought of the different men in her life and was surprised to find that he didn't approve of a single one of them as her lover. Dammit!

Things were moving too fast where Shay was concerned.

Don't be ridiculous, a tiny voice whispered inside his head. You don't really think she's gotten to the age she is and remained a virgin, do you? It was something Kurt had never considered, and was now wishing he'd never begun thinking about in the first place.

"I . . . have certain . . . er . . . feelings for him, but I'm not so sure he returns those feelings."

"I see." Kurt almost gulped in relief. He released her to turn and lean his hips against the work table, his arms crossed over his chest, his expression stern. "I assume you love the man?"

"Oh, no," Shay answered honestly. "But in the last few months I've come to think an affair with him could be fantastic!"

Kurt felt the spasmodic tightening of his stomach muscles. She was dead serious. He wondered why Jane hadn't mentioned anything about this latest development to him. "An affair is serious business, honey." Kurt tried to keep his voice level and controlled. "It certainly isn't something to get involved in without a clear understanding on both sides. There are a number of factors to consider. First . . ."

Shay all but closed her eyes as his voice went on and on about the hazards, the risks involved, the emotional stress, not to mention the time and attention required by both parties. Good grief! she thought disgustedly. He made it sound like an appendectomy!

"Have you found all these things to be true, Kurt?" she asked, managing to stifle her irritation.

His dark eyes studied her, finding incredible delight in the way her eyes gave the barest hint of a slant toward the outer edges. It lent a daring, provocative expression to her face he'd never been aware of before. For the first time he noticed three small freckles on the right side of her nose—a nose that threatened to turn up, but didn't—and the full, laughing curve of her lips.

In the back of his mind he could hear Shay talking, saw her looking at him as if he'd lost his mind, then pointedly glare at him. "Something wrong?" he asked innocently, embarrassed at having been caught gaping at her like some idiot.

"Do you agree?"

"Do I . . ." Kurt looked puzzled and gave a slight shake of his head. "I'm sorry, my mind was wandering." He lifted one hand and rubbed the backs of his fingers across his chin. "What did you say?"

"I was asking you what I should do to try and get this man I mentioned to reveal his feelings a little more. Do you think I should just be honest and tell him how I feel or should I wait?"

"Wait. By all means wait," Kurt said quickly. "By the way," he continued casually, "do I know the guy?"

"I doubt it," Shay innocently replied. "Er . . . he's from out of town."

Kurt thoughtfully digested this bit of information. He told her he would be glad to listen anytime she wanted to talk about her problem, then said good-bye. Shay had to admit that from the little show of emotion she'd seen, Kurt hadn't been overly concerned with her "news." So much for that!

Oh, well. She shrugged philosophically. Nothing ventured, nothing gained. One way or another she knew she would come up with something that would rattle dear ole Kurt's cage—she could feel it in her very bones!

"Your neighbor been giving you a hard time lately?" Jane said as she returned from seeing Kurt out.

"Oh . . ." Shay searched for the right words. "I don't really know how to explain it. Seems lately that everything he does and says annoys me."

"He does tend to be a bit overprotective of you," Jane said thoughtfully. "But then—he's always been that way. I suppose it has something to do with the three of us living next door to each other. You know, we used to make terrible nuisances of ourselves. It's a wonder he didn't drown us."

"Instead, he taught you to swim, but wouldn't allow me in the deep water," Shay said disgustedly. "Mother finally had to say something to him. I wound up taking lessons at the Y."

"Don't judge him too harshly," Jane said softly. "Kurt is a very complex person, Shay. I think he honestly looks upon us as family. We, along with that old harridan Agatha, are the only people he cares about in the entire world. Personally, I think more of the Colonel rubbed off on him than he cares to admit. Basically Kurt is a very caring person, but being raised by that grouchy old man sort of twisted him up emotionally."

"I'm sure you're right." Shay nodded. "But that has nothing to do with the juvenile way he still treats me, Janey. Why, there are times I'm positive he watches my dates bring me home in the evening. There's even been a couple of times in the past few weeks when he's made some remark about how late I got in. Can you beat that!"

Jane threw up her hands and laughed. "I give up. From the looks of things I'd say the two of you are destined to fight. I honestly believe you enjoy baiting each other."

"I don't enjoy it," Shay muttered under her

breath, "but there seems to be little I can do to change it."

"Are you in love with Kurt, Shay?"

The question was sudden, totally unexpected, and threw Shay for a complete loop.

She looked incredulous. "How on earth can you even think such a thing?" she demanded. "We fight like cats and dogs, remember? He thinks I'm still a pigtailed brat. Besides, even if I were so silly as to allow such a thing to happen, I'd be at least sixty before my chance rolled around. You wouldn't believe the way women chase him."

"Oh, yes, I would." Jane grinned. "I still remember some of the things that went on next door when Kurt was holding court."

"Well the game hasn't changed in the least," Shay said scornfully, "but the participants are beginning to look a little jaded." She removed her work gloves, then dusted her hands on the hips of her jeans. "Got time for a cup of coffee?"

" 'Fraid not." Jane smiled. "This is our evening to play bridge. By the time I get home and fix a quick dinner, Ted will be walking in the door."

"Give him and Susie a kiss for me. You might also tell him I'll be coming in to see him professionally. I've been having a toothache lately."

"I'll give him your message, and I'm sorry about the tooth." After kissing her on the cheek and telling her to make a dental appointment first thing the following morning, Jane left.

After a few more minutes of tidying up, Shay locked the greenhouse and headed for a nice leisurely tub bath. She placed her left hand over her right shoulder and tried to reach an aching muscle that felt as if it were being ripped out each time she moved. Darn! She must have strained it earlier lifting those plants. She gritted her teeth and flexed the shoulder anyway, almost groaning aloud at the pain.

"That's all I need," she muttered to herself as she opened the back door and entered the sunny cream-and-blue breakfast room behind the kitchen. Considering the heavy schedule for the remainder of the week, sore shoulder muscles would be a nuisance.

Then she remembered the light-green pills her doctor had given her for the same muscle pull several months ago. She went to the bathroom, started her bath, then found the medication. As she read the directions, she saw that it was to be taken with food. She grimaced, not in the least hungry. She'd eat later, she told herself, then popped two pills into her mouth, followed by a glass of water.

Twenty minutes later Shay was telling herself that she really shouldn't go to sleep in the tub. But for the life of her she couldn't seem to do a single thing about it. The back of her head was resting on a small foam-rubber pillow, and a white froth of bubbles covered the surface of the water. The house was quiet, and even the ringing of the phone hadn't disturbed her. She needed these few minutes to herself, she decided groggily as her neck relaxed and the bottom of her chin dipped below the bubbles.

The next thing she was aware of was strong hands beneath her arms, and the feel of cold air hitting her body as she was hoisted from the now cold water.

The beginnings of a scream were drowned out by Kurt's thundering "Judas priest!" all the while he was subjecting her to a severe shaking. "I've known you to do some damn stupid things before, but this takes the cake. What the hell were you trying to do, kill yourself?"

Though she was still somewhat groggy and her mouth was dry as cotton, Shay took immediate exception to such rough treatment. "Take your damn hands off me!" she cried indignantly.

"Not until you explain a few things," Kurt roared. Shay, having experienced his anger once or twice before, knew what she was in for.

"Take your hands off me," she returned in a low, angry voice, "and get the hell out of this bathroom. I'll explain only if I care to, and only when I'm ready. Unless you're totally blind, you must be aware of the fact that I haven't got on a stitch of clothes." She'd learned long ago that the only way to deal with Kurt and his temper was to stand her ground.

He released her and stepped back, his gaze startled as it ran over the length of her body from head to toe. A rush of color swooped upward from his neck and lent a peculiar ruddy hue to his face beneath his deep tan. He looked toward the marble-topped vanity, snatched up a dark-blue towel, and thrust it at her with the gruff reminder of "You'd better wrap up before you catch cold." He turned abruptly and strode from the steamy bathroom. A few seconds later the door was opened a few inches, and Shay's red robe came sailing toward her.

Kurt walked over to the window of Shay's bedroom, his hands tucked in the back pockets of his pants, while his mind whirled in his head like a merry-go-round. Christ! This was getting out of hand, he lectured himself, something he'd found himself doing almost continuously for the last few days.

Shay Michaels. He said the name over and over in his mind. There certainly wasn't anything different about it. But there sure as hell was something different with the woman who went by that name.

He started to lift a hand to his face, and was surprised to see that it trembled. He uttered a smothered "Damn!," then jammed his hands back in his pockets.

What the hell was wrong with him? Worse yet, what was wrong with Shay? Lately she hadn't been acting at all like herself. He missed the easy camaraderie he'd always shared with her, missed being able to barge into her house or she into his with that special privilege reserved for a relationship such as theirs. They'd always been close, he thought, but lately something had happened. Now there was an edge between them, an angry, invisible line that kept pushing them farther and farther apart. It was as if suddenly one day they had become enemies. He didn't like it, he told himself, didn't like it at all.

The sound of the bathroom door opening brought him out of his reflection and caused him to turn and look at Shay. Her expression was unreadable and even that annoyed Kurt. She'd always been like an open book to him; he'd known her moods and thoughts as well as his own. There'd even been laughing moments when he'd start to say something and she would finish it.

"I'm sorry," he began quietly. "My only excuse is that I was frightened. I'd let your phone ring a number of times. Your van was still parked by the greenhouse, and I hadn't seen you leave with anyone else. I knew your roommate was out of town. Then, when I opened that door"—he nodded toward the bathroom

—"and saw you almost submerged beneath the water, I panicked."

"And after all your lectures not to sleep in the tub." Shay grinned.

"Which apparently went in one ear and out another." Kurt frowned.

"Actually, no," she said softly. "When I finished in the greenhouse, I realized I'd pulled that same darn muscle again in my upper back. I still had some pills left from the last time and I took two of them. I neglected to eat something first, so naturally I was asleep almost as soon as I hit the warm tub."

"Is your back still hurting?" Kurt asked.

"Like the very devil. Lying in that water after it had gotten cold didn't help either." She grimaced.

"Come here and let me massage it for you."

Shay hesitated. Normally she would have bounded over to him without a care in the world, probably jabbering all the while. In fact, she remembered, she *had* done that very same thing before. She'd always been positive Kurt's hands were magic. This time was different, however, and there was a certain hesitancy in her step as she walked over and sat down on the bed next to him.

Kurt saw it but refrained from commenting. Instead, he placed his hands on her shoulders and drew her in front of him. "Put your hands on my waist and lean your head against my

51

chest," he reminded her, "then loosen your robe so I can get my hands beneath the material."

Shay did as he'd instructed, and soon the feel of his capable hands massaging away the pain, and the scent of him swirling about her, had her on an emotional high as lethal as the pills she'd taken.

"Feeling better?" Kurt asked in a husky voice.

"Mmmm," she sighed, the air from her lungs coming in and going out in long, contented breaths. In the midst of that same contentment she realized that her hands no longer were resting on his hips. Instead, her arms were around his waist, and her face was pressed against his chest.

She liked her present position much better, she thought dreamily, much better indeed. It went so much nicer with the way Kurt's wide hands were making those delightful smoothing motions up and down her back.

Suddenly the soft, gentle administrations to her back and shoulders was stilled. Shay felt firm fingers beneath her chin, lifting her face to meet Kurt's enigmatic gaze. She saw it skim her features, then drop to the front of her robe where it gaped open, revealing an uncluttered view of her breasts.

Kurt's hands slid over her shoulders to her upper arms, his grip punishing. "You know

. . ." he said huskily, "you've changed considerably since the days when you used to follow me around, asking twenty questions a minute. You were a runt of a tomboy then, and always looking for a fight."

"Tha—that's because I was forced to wear those hateful braces and those ugly glasses," she whispered in spite of her tongue feeling an inch thick, and her heart running away with her.

Before she had time to prepare herself for what was happening, Shay felt his hand release its hold on her arm and then move to cup the slight fullness of one breast in his palm. But before she could savor the moment or begin to deal with the incredible pleasure he was giving her, Kurt jerked his hands away from her as if he'd been burned and stood up abruptly.

Without thinking, Shay pulled the edges of her robe together. His actions left her with a river of unfulfilled desire running rampant within her, but at the same time caused her to be ashamed.

"I'm sorry," he muttered stiffly, silently hating himself. "I shouldn't have touched you like that," he finally offered after a lengthy silence. He heard himself apologizing for something that had happened as naturally as breathing, something he'd been thinking of for weeks now. But rather than enjoying caressing the body of a lovely woman, Kurt felt torn between his suddenly seeing Shay for the first time as a sexy woman, and his protective instincts that had always guarded and taken care of her. To be perfectly candid, he decided, he felt like a first-class bastard!

His voice was rigid and clipped, and Shay would have liked nothing better than to knock him over the head with a baseball bat! "No," she muttered on a long, exhaled breath, "I don't suppose you should have." She shoved her hands into the pockets of the robe, and continued to stare at him. "But just for the record, why shouldn't you?"

Kurt's eyes grew wide with shock. He was quiet for a moment, then frowned. "Why shouldn't I—what?"

"Kiss me—make love to me. Treat me like you would any other woman. Assuming, of course, that you don't find me totally repugnant."

"That's the silliest damn statement I've ever heard you make," he said roughly. He ran a hand through his hair, leaving it in comical spikes.

"Tell me why it's silly," Shay persisted, suddenly finding his reaction to the last five minutes exasperating, while at the same time highly amusing. An unsure Kurt was something to behold.

"Well, because . . ." he floundered, gesturing with his large hands and shaking his head. "Because . . . you're Shay," he announced, as if that alone put her in a class labeled "Untouchable." "Already I'm feeling like I've sunk lower than a snake's belly by even thinking of touching you—much less actually doing so—and you have the nerve to ask me why I haven't tried to get you into my bed."

Shay gritted her teeth. Men were stupid in general, but standing before her was the master of them all.

A wide smile of satisfaction curved Shay's lips. "You mean you've actually been thinking of making love to me, Kurt?"

"Yes!" he snapped.

"Good. I was beginning to think you were blind."

"I'm not blind"—he glared at her—"and I don't see a damn thing 'good' about it." He swung about and strode toward the door. "From now on, make sure you don't go to sleep in the bathtub," he threw over his shoulder, his voice cruel and rough.

Shay stood up slowly, listening to his progress through the house and out the back door. Okay, she quietly lectured herself, so she'd blown that round. Don't worry, there would be other opportunities to open her neighbor's eyes. . . .

CHAPTER THREE

Kurt cursed himself the entire time it took him to walk from Shay's house to his.

Of all the damn stupid things to have done, he kept repeating. He'd known Shay practically all her life. He was fourteen years older than she was, and he felt like some lowlife with no morals at all.

When he burst through the back door and stormed through the spacious kitchen, Maggie, his housekeeper, regarded his stormy features and then his quickly retreating back with calm resignation.

She knew without even asking that Shay Michaels was responsible for Kurt's dark mood. Maggie wondered, as she went on about her task of preparing dinner, just when it would hit the foolish man that he was head over heels in love with Shay. She wondered what would happen to Kurt if she weren't there to cook and clean for him. Would he venture next door for an occasional sandwich? Would Shay feel it her "duty" to offer to come over and fix dinner once in a while?

She dropped the potholder onto the counter, crossed her fingers, and went in search of Kurt, finding him in the library standing before the French doors, nursing a Scotch and water. "I'm going to visit my sister for a couple of weeks," Maggie announced in her blunt fashion.

"When?"

"Tomorrow."

Kurt turned at her. "Don't you think your notice leaves a lot to be desired—timewise?" he asked sarcastically.

Maggie shrugged. She was blunt, outspoken, and had worked for Kurt for nearly ten years. "Frankly, I haven't given it much thought." She turned and started to leave the room. "I'll leave you a few things in the freezer to eat while I'm gone," she threw over her shoulder. "If you get hungry enough, you can always get Shay to fix you something. She's not a bad cook."

Kurt's loud "Humph!" was his only response. He turned back to stare broodingly through the square panes of glass. Go to Shay's to eat indeed! She would probably poison him, he thought disgustedly.

Well, she certainly didn't have poisoning you in mind earlier, his conscience said mockingly, which only served to make Kurt blanch at the thought of what had taken place, and what it could have turned into if he hadn't put the brakes on. He slowly shook his head, feeling like a jerk. Shay had always trusted him. He'd fixed toys for her, comforted her through numerous skinned knees, and had even been the chauffeur for her and Billy Jasper on the occasion of her first dance.

His mind became a kaleidoscope of Shays, ranging from infancy to the present—clothed and as he'd seen her not quite thirty minutes ago. Kurt groaned. His thoughts were driving him crazy.

He'd stay away from her, he promised himself as he struggled to gain some semblance of control over his thoughts. He'd stay away and in time maybe they could regain the old relationship they'd enjoyed for so many years.

But what about the things she said to you? a small voice asked. She sounded as if she wasn't sorry for what happened. Doesn't that give you reason to believe that you're being just a wee bit unfair to yourself? Not at all, Kurt immediately answered his own question, it was infatuation. He was convinced what Shay was feeling for him was infatuation. She'd had a crush on him since she was in the second grade.

The next morning as Kurt, his eyes bloodshot from lack of sleep and too much Scotch and his temper on an incredibly short string, backed his dark-blue Mercedes out of the garage, he glanced over the hedgerow and caught a glimpse of Shay just opening the door of the van. Without thinking, Kurt let the window down and yelled, "How's the shoulder this morning?"

All he got for his friendly effort was to be glacially ignored. His head whipped around as his eyes followed the tan van out the drive next door and as it slipped into the early-morning traffic.

"What the hell's she so upset about?" he muttered, gunning the engine of the Mercedes and flying backward like a bat out of hell. "I'm the one with the million-dollar guilt trip!"

In seconds he'd cut into traffic, and soon eased in behind the van. He rode the center lane, determined to let the driver of the van know that she was being followed.

Shay gripped the steering wheel with both hands, her lips compressed in a straight, annoyed line. Kurt Barron had just as good as told her last night to drop dead, she thought rebelliously, so why was he trailing along behind her with an expression as dark as a storm?

For a while last night she'd considered other, more obvious ways in which to go after dear old Kurt. But after carefully examining each of them, Shay decided her best plan would be to ignore him.

"Which looks as if it's going to be easier said than done," she muttered when they rode past the street where his offices were located. Apparently he wasn't satisfied with having insulted her last night, he seemed to want another crack at it this morning. "Oh, well." She grinned evilly. "If it makes him happy, who am I to argue?"

She suddenly flipped on her right-hand blinker, then whipped into the parking lot of a large bank. But she hadn't been fast enough. Before Shay could get her feet to the ground, the door of the van was jerked open and a grim-faced Kurt was standing before her, his balled fists jammed on his hips, his expression anything but friendly.

"What the hell's wrong with you this morning?" he demanded, totally disregarding the interested stares of several of the bank employees making their way inside. "You flew out of that damned driveway doing ninety miles an hour. Last night you tried to drown yourself. This morning you try making an airplane of this van. Are you trying to kill yourself?"

"Well—my goodness, it's Kurt. What a surprise," Shay chirped with saccharine sweetness. "Early-morning banking appointment?"

"I'm waiting for an answer to my question, Shay," he said determinedly.

Shay sat back in the seat, realizing that until she gave him some sort of satisfaction, her chances of getting through, over, or around him were nil. "I thought we set the new guidelines for our relationship last night."

"What the hell is that supposed to mean?" Kurt demanded. He pulled at the collar of his white shirt, and even flexed his broad shoulders beneath the dark material of the impeccably tailored suit. Could it possibly be that Kurt Barron was nervous? Shay wondered.

"Why, Kurt—don't you remember?" She smiled frostily. "After the positively *scandalous* way you acted last night, you turned into a hypocritical tyrant and stormed out of my house. Naturally I assumed you wouldn't want to be embarrassed by having me shower you with my usual gushy greeting."

"There was nothing hypocritical about the way I acted, nor were my actions that scandalous," he snapped.

"Really?" Shay purred. "Then you did enjoy those few intimate moments between us? You aren't sorry it happened? Your words, not mine," she added facetiously.

"Of course I'm sorry it happened," he countered in a loud voice that caused passersby to stare curiously at him. "That is"—he gestured wildly with his hands—"There was something between us at that particular moment that made me lose control. I spent most of the night thinking of a solution. It would seem to me the most sensible thing for us to do is not see each other for a while."

"Good." After uttering that one word of agreement Shay slipped down from the driv-

61

er's seat of the van and around Kurt's mountain of a body.

Kurt followed her to the back of the van, his expression one of disbelief at how quickly she'd agreed with his plan. Perhaps he was wrong in his assumption that she still secretly nourished a crush on him. Could be she'd gotten over it, he pondered. Of course, he suddenly decided. He was the father figure in her life—father, brother, and sweetheart all rolled into one. It was natural for her to try out her feminine wiles on him.

A new surge of confidence swept over Kurt, and he gazed fondly down at Shay as she placed the lightweight collapsible cart on the ground and began adding the different things she would need for the plants inside the bank. Last night had been a bad mistake on his part. Now that he recognized the situation for what it really was, he was sure he and Shay would be able to continue along as they always had.

"It didn't take you long to agree with my suggestion," he said cajolingly. He reached out and brushed the tips of his fingers along the line of her jaw, her skin soft and smooth to his touch. "Are you that anxious to get rid of me?"

"Yes." Shay turned so that she was out of his reach and then pushed the cart between them. "Excuse me, Kurt. I have several stops to make this morning."

Kurt stood like a statue, watching her small,

shapely body cross the parking lot and enter the bank without a backward look. Dammit to hell! he swore violently. She'd acted like she was thrilled to death with his suggestion. He turned on his heel and stalked to where the Mercedes was parked and got in. As the engine purred to life and the car left the parking lot, Kurt was angrily gripping the wheel with both hands. He was driving purely from instinct, his thoughts on his maddening neighbor.

What the hell was the matter with him? he wondered with fierce disapproval. What on earth had made him act like a complete ass by even trying to talk with her in the first place? So stay away from her, his personal irritating voice threw at him. But Kurt knew that the advice—though possibly the best he would ever get—seemed impossible to take. A future without Shay in it appeared bleak. Too bleak even to consider.

Ian Deaton leaned back in his chair and pulled on his pipe, his pudgy fingers lovingly caressing the shiny bowl. He was a short, stocky individual, with a sunny disposition that made people trust him on sight. A factor that proved invaluable in his particular occupation. He ran his free hand through the thinning gray hair on his head, his shrewd gaze traveling about the cold, impersonal motel room with obvious distaste.

This type of living was one of the many hazards of his profession. It kept one away from one's comfortable home and a toasty fire on cold evenings. It also made one's wife more than a little angry when she discovered her husband had agreed to go out on an assignment when he'd promised her two years ago that he wouldn't go farther from home than the grocery store. Ian had worked long and hard to get in a position of picking and choosing the cases he took. He employed five topnotch investigators and was thinking of taking on another one. So why are you sitting here in this godforsaken place? he asked himself.

Because—Ian smiled, pleased—getting the opportunity to work for Nicholas Pappolas had been too much to pass up. Especially after Ian had listened to the man's story. He was a likable cuss, and Ian had immediately decided he would handle the case personally.

Now here he sat in a small motel in an even smaller town in Nevada, looking for a woman who apparently didn't want to be found, and who quite probably was the mother of Nicholas Pappolas's only heir. Interesting, Ian mused, very interesting. And it would prove even more so if the news media ever got wind of the story. He'd have to be extra careful in that direction. For the price Nicholas Pappolas was paying, he certainly deserved his privacy.

He picked up a single sheet of paper from

the small round table beside his chair and studied it. So far he'd encountered only negative responses to his inquiries. The address unearthed by the detective Nicholas had hired years ago, no longer existed. A large apartment complex stood in the area. Ian pursed his lips as he continued to peruse the information at hand. Marie Connors, Emily's good friend who had sat with the ailing husband, was dead. Old newspapers from the library revealed nothing about Emily Crawford's automobile accident and, fourteen months later, her husband's death as a result of complications arising from that accident.

Ian let the sheet of paper flutter downward to the table, his brow furrowed thoughtfully. According to the paper John Crawford had been the victim in the accident. That being the case, Ian concluded, it would mean—if there was insurance involved—that a trust fund would have been set up for any minor Crawford child. Ian looked back at the obit notice . . . yes, there had been one child, as mentioned by Nicholas Pappolas.

With an extra spring in his movements Ian rose quickly to his feet and began pacing the room. He'd try to track down the records for a trust fund for the minor child. And possibly for the unborn child as well? he murmured. The question was immediately quashed. Ian figured that any woman whose husband had been in a comatose state for months, would hardly try to negotiate a trust fund for an unborn child by another man . . . although legally the child—if there was one—would have belonged to John Crawford.

He couldn't help but wonder how Emily Crawford handled that sticky little situation. Though after his trip to the courthouse the next day, he mused, he should have an answer to his question.

Shay stared at the mangled fender and front grill of the van, still unable to believe that she'd done such a stupid thing. She'd driven over this same stretch of highway almost every day of her life. Suddenly, today, she forgot about a hard curve, found herself unable to make the turn, and wound up with the front of the van crunched against a tall pine.

The uniformed officer looked up from his task of taking down her account of what had happened. "Are you sure you're all right, Miss Michaels? You look pale, and that bump on your head is getting larger. You've also got a nasty bruise on your elbow."

"I'm okay, Officer." She smiled thinly. "I'm sure once I get over the shock I'll be fine."

The sound of a car screaming to a halt, the door slamming, and rapid footsteps approaching, brought a halt to any further conversation at the moment. Even without looking up Shay knew who the person was.

There was a wild look on Kurt's face when he jerked open the door on the passenger side of the officer's car. The full brunt of his gaze rested on Shay, the depth of its intensity probing her very soul. "Shay?" His voice carried a decided wobble that melted the iciness of her heart. He was concerned, and she couldn't thumb her nose at such feelings.

"I'm all right, Kurt," she said gently.

He looked from her to the officer. "Is she finished here?"

"I think so." The officer smiled. "If we need anything else, we can get in touch later. If I were you, I'd run her by the emergency room. She insists she's all right, but I really think she should be X-rayed."

Shay opened her mouth to protest, but found herself being lifted in Kurt's arms and carried to the Mercedes. "You do realize that the people in every car that goes by are staring at us, don't you?"

"Who the hell cares?" he said roughly.

"Who indeed." She sighed, leaning her aching head against his chest. She would argue later. At the moment she was too tired to care. Kurt, on the other hand, had other ideas.

"Did you get a good look at the joker who forced you off the road?" he asked the moment he slid behind the wheel. It was beginning to get dark, and the dimness cast interesting shadows against his rough features.

"No one ran me off the road, Kurt. I lost control of the van."

"You did what?" he came close to shouting as he barreled down the highway toward the hospital.

"I lost control," she slowly repeated as if speaking to someone slow to grasp the simplest words. "One minute I was driving along like I normally do, and the next thing I know, I'm heading toward that damn tree like shot from a gun. I couldn't seem to turn the steering wheel."

"You were driving too damned fast," she was told in a gruff voice. "I've talked till I'm blue in the face, but you refuse to listen. You drive like a damned maniac," he threw at her as he turned into the emergency entrance on two wheels and came to a screeching stop.

"Really?" Shay remarked, her lips quivering humorously in spite of her pain.

For once Kurt appeared at a loss for words. He half turned in the seat, one hand reaching out and cupping her nape. "I almost died when I turned that curve back there and saw your van smashed up, honey. The thought of something happening to you is more than I can stand."

Shay positively glowed under the reflection of feeling in his dark eyes. *At last,* she all but sighed, *at last*. Kurt was finally looking at her for what she was . . . a woman. Her aching head and her bum elbow were more than worth the effort if it had brought him to his senses.

"You and Janey are the only family I've got." He smiled. "You're like the sister I never knew."

The smile on Shay's face froze. Dear Lord! she prayed. Please give me strength not to kill him!

"Let's go on in, shall we?" she said shortly, trying to control her anger.

Kurt looked at her knowingly as he helped her out of the car and into the emergency room. He felt like three kinds of a heel, but he'd seen the glowing look of adoration in her eyes when he'd blubbered on like an idiot. He'd known then that he had to do something to bring her back down to earth. He was confident that in time she would thank him for not taking advantage of her innocence.

Later, after insisting on fixing her a light supper of soup and a sandwich, Kurt saw her to bed. "Don't worry, I'll be sleeping in the room next door," he promised.

"But you really don't need to do that," Shay said politely. Secretly she was delighted. Who knew what could happen if she were to have a nightmare during the night?

"Nonsense," he shushed her. "Do you think

I'd leave you on your own? You aren't that seriously injured, but the doctor suggested that someone be with you for this one night in the event of shock, and since Janey's got the flu, that leaves me."

He bent to brush his lips against her cheek, but Shay turned her head at the last second and his lips landed smack against hers. At first she was afraid he was going to jerk away again. But to her surprise he didn't. She felt the edge of the bed give as he eased his body down, then felt his arms slipping around her, crushing her against his massive chest.

His tongue glided against the smoothness of her lips, then sought the secrets awaiting him in that darkened paradise beyond. The sensitive tip savored the taste of her mouth even as he fought to dispel the cloud of unbelievable headiness swirling around them and threatening the very existence of everything Kurt had been fighting for these past few weeks. If only Shay would help him, he thought wildly, but even at the thought, he had to smile. God! She was responding to him more beautifully than he'd ever imagined.

His hands were gentle, caressing her with long, sweeping strokes of bridled passion. He wanted to crush her and absorb her within his being, and yet, he knew a kind of love for her that made him want to handle her with the same care and devotion one accorded delicate porcelain.

Tears made their escape beneath Shay's closed lids as the emotion of being in Kurt's arms and having him kiss and caress her began to penetrate the incredibly beautiful world into which she'd been suddenly thrust. She couldn't possibly let herself think for a moment on the future. Instead she would concentrate on the present . . . and enjoy.

"Oh, Shay! Shay, baby," he murmured as his lips left hers and rested against her hair. "You're tearing me up inside, do you know that?" He eased her back so that he could look into her eyes. "It would be so easy to take advantage of the situation, sweetheart, but I can't."

"You wouldn't be taking advantage, Kurt," she told him in a quiet voice. "For the life of me I can't figure out why you're so blind where I'm concerned. We're each of age and consenting adults. What's there to keep us from enjoying each other?"

"I want you to be sure, Shay," he said sternly, then tempered the remark by smiling. "Honey, I'm not unfamiliar with the way you've always felt about me. That being the case, I honestly think you've allowed your emotions to run away with you. You want me now, but in a few months an affair could be an embarrassing memory you'd rather forget."

"Never," Shay softly vowed.

Kurt sighed, shaking his head defeatedly. "Try it my way"—he threw up his hand when she started to speak—"for six months. Let's be friends, even go out with each other occasionally . . . but no heavy stuff. If you still feel the same way at the end of that time, then we'll see what happens."

CHAPTER FOUR

Shay had agreed that night . . . and she'd regretted it. On the other hand, she told herself, she'd had very little choice in the matter.

She touched cologne to her throat and at her wrist, then studied her reflection in the mirror. The soft yellow dress suited her mood perfectly. She lifted her stubborn chin higher and stared at the revealing neckline. She wondered what Kurt would think about it.

Don't worry about what he thinks about it, she told herself. You're going with him to Agatha's simply because the old woman expects it of you. And you will continue to go as long as she requests you to do so.

But going to Agatha's meant going with Kurt, and since that night of the wreck, Shay and Kurt had avoided each other like the plague.

Don't be a child, she flared. If he annoys you that much, then put on a blindfold and stuff your ears with cotton. But don't bring tacky feuds into your friendship with Agatha. She's old. She's lonely. Humor her.

Tomorrow evening, which was Friday, she had a date with Wes Pollock. On Saturday evening she was seeing Max Wingate, and on Sunday, it was Roger Denison. If that wasn't enough to keep her mind off Kurt, then she'd run a damned ad in the newspaper!

When the doorbell sounded, Shay stood in the middle of the living room for a full sixty seconds without moving in an attempt to bolster her courage. She'd seen Kurt only once in the week since the wreck, and that had been just a wave over the fence. During that time they'd gone to great lengths to stay out of each other's way. Even knowing she needed some sort of temporary transportation hadn't swayed Kurt, and Shay knew then that the break was for real. Ordinarily he'd have had some sort of vehicle at her door the next morning, plus given her an hour-long lecture. None of it had happened, and for Shay, life had been quite lonely of late.

With her head held high she walked to the door and opened it, bracing herself for the initial shock of Kurt's staggering gaze. She wasn't disappointed, the effects almost floored her. She gripped the doorknob till her knuckles were white, willing her face into a pleasant mask of politeness.

He drew in a slow, deep breath. "Hello,

honey," he drawled huskily, his voice warming her, his eyes caressing her as if physically touching her. He was totally devastating in gray pants and a charcoal blazer, Shay acknowledged, not that she'd expected him to undergo some drastic changes in a few days.

But she could hope, couldn't she, that there would be the tiniest show of absence having made his heart grow fonder as well as having added a few distinguishing lines to his face?

"Kurt." She nodded, just friendly enough. She picked up a light coat from a chair close to the door, reached for her purse, then turned back to face him. "Shall we go?"

She had taken only two steps before she felt Kurt's hand drop to her arm and stop her. "You're looking exceptionally lovely tonight," he murmured gruffly.

"Paying each other compliments wasn't in the rules you created for the next six months, Kurt. Remember?" She stared straight ahead, more out of fear he'd see how his touch brought a special brightness to her eyes or how her hands, had they not been clutching her purse, would be trembling.

"Very well," Kurt snapped. He palmed her elbow and hustled her from her house, across the side yard to his car. "I won't declare you a traitor if you smile," he threw in as he opened the passenger door for her, "and if you don't want . . . er . . . compliments"—he grinned evilly—"then I suggest you wear something a little less revealing the next time we visit Agatha."

Less revealing indeed! Shay silently seethed as she sat stiff as a board in the passenger seat. To Kurt, any neckline an inch below her collarbone was revealing. At least he'd been courteous enough to compliment her on how well she looked this evening, she fumed, even if it had been merely a perfunctory gesture on his part. As for revealing, she thought, continuing to nurse her anger, she'd like to "reveal" something to him, all right, but it certainly wasn't her cleavage. She had something more forceful in mind—like, perhaps, dynamiting his brain!

Another thing that irritated her was the way he'd tried to turn on the charm back there in her living room, as if he'd thought she was expecting it. She'd fallen for that trick in the emergency room, and had been mortified to hear him switch gears in the middle of his conversation and begin going on about how she and Jane were like his sisters . . . the family he'd never had.

"Your roommate still away?" Kurt broke the testy silence after several glances at Shay's profile.

"She'll be back any time now," she stiffly replied, then clammed up. She didn't want to talk to him. It was wasted effort.

Kurt fought to keep a straight face in light of

her deliberate frostiness. "Did you have a good day?"

"Yes."

"Tell me about it?"

Shay threw him a withering look, then resumed staring straight ahead. "I started off the day by watering and fertilizing the plants in your reception bay, then made a stop by Dr. Thompson's and one at Ted's."

Kurt frowned. "I thought tomorrow was the date for doing whatever it is you do to my plants." He'd be willing to bet any amount of money that she'd reworked her schedule around the times he would be out of the office, as he'd been this morning.

"It's not a matter of life or death that I keep to the exact date," she said stiffly. "Don't worry, if any of the plants suffer, I'll see to it that your account is credited with the appropriate adjustment."

"Need I tell you what you can do with your 'appropriate adjustment'?" he said roughly. He didn't want some damn credit to his account, he thought, scowling.

"Well, really, Kurt." Shay pretended to be highly insulted. Inwardly she was pleased that she'd pierced his thick hide. "Must you be so crude?"

"Hell, yes." He shot her a quelling glare. "I will be crude or nasty or whatever else comes to mind when I find out that you choose to visit my office only when you know I'm away. I resent that, Shay."

She turned and met his angry gaze. "That's too bad, Kurt. But if it bothers you that much, then I'll be glad to find someone else to take over the care of your plants."

"Do what you feel you must," he surprised Shay by replying. "But I really don't think I would if I were you."

"And why not?" she immediately asked, ready to go the direct opposite of his opinion, regardless of what that opinion was.

"Because I'd be forced to take out a large ad in the local paper," he said smoothly.

"An ad for what?"

"To let your other customers know that the contracts they've signed with you are about as worthless as the paper they're drawn up on."

"That's blackmail."

"So it is." Kurt shrugged. "And so, you'll have to make a decision. Won't you?"

"Such as?"

"Such as don't make threats about dropping me as one of your customers. I like having you tend that damned jungle you've created through my entire office complex. It's . . ." he hesitated, as if embarrassed. "It's rather nice."

"Ha!" Shay hooted derisively. "That's a laugh. On the other hand, coming from you, I suppose it could be looked upon as some sort of left-field compliment, considering you positively detest plants."

"I've gotten used to them," Kurt said blandly, a devilish gleam in his eyes and a persuasive twist softening his mouth. He saw the haunted look that had been present in Shay's eyes from the moment she'd opened the door to him beginning to recede. Good, Kurt thought. He was tired of arguing, especially when all he wanted to do was take her in his arms and make love to her. He could still feel the gleaming softness of her breast in his hand, and could still see the diamond-hard tip inviting his caresses.

Shay looked at Kurt and frowned. "You'd better slow down, we're almost there." The least he could do was pay attention, she fumed.

"I'm sorry." He threw her a confused glance. "What did you say?"

"We're going to Agatha's for dinner, remember?" she sternly reminded him. "You'd better put on brakes or we'll miss the turn."

Kurt pulled at the corner of his bottom lip, a look of chagrin on his face. God! If he didn't keep his thoughts under control, he would kill them with his stupid carelessness.

Damn him! Shay thought angrily. She didn't know what to make of him. One minute he was caressing her with that deep, velvety voice of his and the next thing she knew, he was as cold and distant as an iceberg.

Lillie, the cook and housekeeper who had been with Agatha Crosby forever, didn't appear any different than she had from the first moment Shay could remember her. Of medium height, with salt-and-pepper hair caught at the nape in a neat twist, Lillie gave the appearance of being ageless.

"Have you any idea how old she is?" Shay whispered to Kurt as they followed the ramrod-straight individual down a wide, spacious hall to some distant room Agatha had chosen at the moment for her "little corner."

"Methuselah's sister at least," Kurt murmured out of the corner of his mouth. "Agatha is older than God."

"Amen," Shay whispered as they were shown into a long, narrow room that had obviously been redecorated since Shay's last visit.

Shay glanced around, nodding approvingly at the large windows, and immediately fell in love with the wallpaper of tiny yellow flowers on a cream background. Wicker furniture painted the same soft cream color was scattered comfortably about. Parquet flooring gave off a lustrous gleam and was a perfect foil for several large green plants in ceramic and brass planters. It was a striking room that immediately made one feel welcome.

Shay often wondered how Agatha, who was known for her sharp tongue and general contrariness, could exhibit such warmth and airiness when it came to decorating . . . which the older woman did with such regularity, it had become a joke among most of her acquaintances and friends.

"It's about time," a sharp voice spoke abruptly from the far end of the room. "You should buy yourself a new watch, Kurtland. The one you're now wearing obviously isn't worth a tinker's damn."

The corners of Shay's mouth turned up as she spotted the tiny birdlike figure of Agatha, sitting in a high-backed wicker chair and—as best Shay could make out—dressed in a caftan-like garment in brillant hues of greens and blues. Her snow-white hair was piled on top of her small head, and her famous diamonds were everywhere . . . around her neck, at her wrists, and on her fingers. To Shay, Agatha looked like the queen she remembered conjuring up during her childhood daydreams when her mother would read her fairy tales.

"Shay. It's so good of you to come," the dictatorial voice, which always seemed so at odds with Agatha's size, continued. "For the life of me I can't understand why you don't drop by on your own. I've always been rather fond of you, child. We do have several things that need discussing, and Kurtland's presence keeps me from being able to speak freely to you."

"I'm sorry, Agatha." Shay smiled as she drew to a stop in front of the old lady, then bent and touched her lips to the gently lined cheek. Agatha smelled of lavender, Shay thought pleasantly as she straightened and stepped aside for Kurt to greet his aunt. "I'll make it a point to do better. I also promise to leave . . . er . . . Kurtland home the next time I come."

"See that you do, young lady. Kurtland," Agatha said softly. There was love in her blue eyes, eyes that weren't quite as deeply blue or glowing as they had been ninety years before, but keenly sharp just the same.

"Aunt Agatha," Kurt drawled in that raspy manner that was as much a part of him as the air he breathed. The sound of it warmed Shay inside. He smiled down at the tiny figure of his aunt, then bent and kissed her the same as Shay had done, though he lingered in front of her, holding one of her fragile hands in his larger one. "You're looking exceptionally lovely this evening."

"What did you expect?" she asked archly. "A walker and a hearing aid?"

"Perish the thought." Kurt chuckled. He released her hand, but waited till Shay was seated in one of the two chairs drawn to the right and left of Agatha, but facing her, then took his own seat. "Anything exciting been happening since I saw you last?"

"I've had Mr. Corstaires over for dinner."

"Is that suppose to be exciting?" Kurt teased.

"When you're ninety-odd years old, young

man, everything that happens in the course of a day is exciting," Agatha said sternly. "As for Mr. Corstaires, I'm not so sure. I'd thought of seeing more of him, but I've decided he's too old."

"Exactly how old is the gentleman, Agatha?" Shay asked curiously.

"Eighty-five."

"Oh."

"I've always preferred younger men, dear. On the other hand"—she lifted her regal head and sharply regarded Shay—"there are other cases where a woman is happier with a man older than she is. Such as you and Kurtland. The difference in your ages makes you quite suitable for each other."

This little speech fell in the midst of the trio like a lead balloon. Shay could feel the red rising from her throat to cover her face completely in a hot cloud of embarrassment.

Kurt's gaze became flinty as he regarded his elderly relative.

"No comment?" Agatha chuckled, immensely pleased with herself.

"Shay is seeing several other men at this particular time," Kurt said smoothly. "I'm afraid she hasn't time for old friends. Why, last night it was nearly one o'clock before she came home."

"And just how would you know what time I got in?" Shay "sweetly" countered. "Wasn't

83

Tessa entertaining enough for you, or did you become bored and leave early?"

Agatha's small head was turning from right to left with unbelievable interest.

"As usual, Tessa was the perfect hostess," Kurt replied with syrupy politeness. The slightest emphasis on the last two words had Shay's fingernails digging into her palms.

Kurt turned to Agatha and shrugged. "As you can see, we're both rather busy—with other 'things.' Personally, I would be happy to spend more time with my charming neighbor." He smiled warmly at Shay, though his eyes were as hard as nails. "But there just doesn't seem to be any way for us to get together. And even if we could manage it, we each have other interests now. There's nothing more boring than attempting to resurrect an old relationship that's become something of a habit."

"So I see," the old woman said slowly, staring accusingly down her tiny nose at Shay.

Oh, no, you don't, Shay thought determinedly, even as she was smarting from the remark—especially the word *boring*. That hurt. However, she wasn't about to let Kurt get away with turning his ill-tempered relative on her. "Actually, Agatha," she began smiling with false indulgence, "Kurt, as usual, is being modest. He's so popular, you know. I'm afraid he's the one who doesn't have time for me.

Why, it wasn't more than a couple of weeks ago that I actually heard a woman simply begging him to make time for her in his busy schedule. Can you imagine that? About the only time he's able to see me at all is when we're to have dinner with you. But . . . what can I say?" she added on a resigned note. Now wiggle out of that, you twerp!

"Is that so?" Agatha quipped. She glared at Kurt. "Would you mind checking the faucet in my bathroom? It's been leaking for several days now."

"Of course," he murmured silkily as he rose to his formidable height. "Why else did I drive halfway across town except to fix a leaky faucet?" He pinned Shay with a piercing glare. "Don't be telling dear Aunt Agatha any more of our 'little secrets.' " Then he turned on his heel and walked away.

Agatha watched him leave the room with an expression on her face that strongly reminded Shay of a fat cat about to pounce on a helpless bird!

"How's that sister of yours?"

Shay gave a slight start at the suddenness of the question. "Jane and her family are fine, Agatha." She smiled. "She sends you her regards," Shay lied without a hitch.

"Hmph," snorted the older woman. "I still can't figure out what she saw in that dentist when she could have had Kurtland."

"It's simple, Agatha," Shay said firmly. "She and Kurt didn't love each other." A sudden thought occurred to Shay. "Has anyone ever told you the real story of that engagement?"

"What's there to tell?" Agatha spread her hands dramatically. "She *had* a bird in the hand and wanted the two in the bush as well."

It was all Shay could do to keep from laughing as she imagined Jane's face when she heard herself described in such unflattering terms. "My sister didn't jilt Kurt in the traditional sense, Agatha. They were only engaged because he agreed to help Jane."

"Help her? How?"

"As I'm sure you know, my mother had— certain ideas about the men she wanted as husbands for Jane and me."

"Rich." Agatha uttered the one word and Shay grinned.

"Correct. I can't say I agreed with her, but that's neither here nor there. At any rate, presumably she picked out a young man for my sister. Jane rebelled. As my mother applied her own particular type of pressure, Jane went to Kurt and told him what was happening. They decided the best way to put an end to Mother's meddling was for them to pretend to be engaged. Shortly afterward Jane met Ted, and you know the rest."

"What an admirable thing for Kurtland to

do," Agatha remarked, her blue gaze challenging.

"If you say so." Shay lifted one shoulder indifferently. "On the other hand, I think Jane acted in very good faith. As wealthy as Kurt is, she could have created some unpleasant publicity over the broken engagement. She could also have kept the ring she wore for those three months."

"If *you* say so," Agatha mimicked. "Now, let's talk about your business. How is it coming along?"

"Very nicely. The rental business is super, and this morning I even had to turn down a new customer. I haven't regretted for a single moment opening up my own shop."

"You have determination, Shay, the same kind of determination I want in Kurtland's wife. You'd do well, my dear, to set your sights on him," Agatha advised. "He's rich, sexy, and I happen to know you've always followed him around like a puppy dog. It's not impossible for a childish crush to turn into true love, you know."

"I'll keep that in mind," Shay coolly returned just as Lillie appeared in the doorway and announced that dinner was ready.

Shay stood on one side of the chair, with the housekeeper on the other, as Agatha slowly rose to her feet. The three of them moved slowly toward the dining room. There they were joined by Kurt, who came in easing his arms back into his jacket.

"You need new washers for that faucet, Aunt Agatha," he informed her as he seated her at the head of the table. Shay quickly took her seat before he could assist her, an action that brought a grin of amusement to Kurt's face. He could easily see by the set of her lips that she was displeased. "Better still"—he turned back to his aunt—"why don't you call a plumber?"

"Because all they do is piddle around for hours on end and then charge you an exorbitant amount of money. Two days later the faucet will be leaking again. I'll have Lillie get the washers. The next time you stop by, you can fix the sink."

The meal progressed to dessert before Agatha resumed her matchmaking comments. "Have you been to Phoenix lately?" she innocently asked Kurt.

"Yesterday. I'm thinking of building a shopping center there. Why?" he asked. "Do you need me to tend to some business for you down there?"

"No," she murmured. "It's just that I was wondering how long it's been since you took Shay to the ballet. I understand they'll be performing *Swan Lake* for another week." She turned to Shay. "Wouldn't you like to see *Swan Lake?*"

"I've seen it three times," she replied in a flat

voice. She just couldn't concentrate on the conversation. Kurt had actually had the nerve to call their relationship boring and Shay felt as though she'd suddenly lost something very special in her life. She threw a surreptitious glance toward Kurt, her eyes finding pleasure in simply watching him. He was so vital. Excitement shot off him like sparks from an electrical current, transmitting itself to the people around him and encompassing them in his own special force-field. Yet, as much as she enjoyed the sight of him, Shay also became aware of a deep aching in her chest.

Have you lost something? her conscience mocked her.

Shay felt like crying. Oh, yes, she told herself, she'd lost something. She'd just had a childhood fantasy shattered, and she'd have much preferred letting it slip slowly from her grasp in her own sweet time to having it snatched away so brutally.

"More wine, Shay?"

Shay glanced up at the sound of her name, her gaze meeting and locking with Kurt's. "No, thank you," she said softly, her expression a mixture of sadness and something else he was unable to read.

An eerie iciness scampered over Kurt's flesh as he stared at her. If he knew his Shay, he would judge she'd just undergone a mood swing of at least one hundred and eighty degrees . . . and Kurt wondered what it was all about.

Shortly after dinner Shay pleaded a headache and asked Kurt to take her home. "Care to talk about it?" he asked once they were in the car and on their way.

"I beg your pardon?"

"Whatever it is that seems to be bothering you. You pretty much ran the gamut of emotions this evening. I saw you amused, angry, disgusted, and now sad. What happened to bring about the sadness? Or perhaps I should ask, what did I do?"

Shay turned and stared thoughtfully at him, as if seeing him for the first time. There was so much of Kurt. She wondered if she would ever see a tall, broad-shouldered man again without thinking of him. "What makes you so sure you're responsible?" she asked with a sting in her voice. "In case you've forgotten, your aunt is rather outspoken, and we have spent the last two and a half hours with her."

"The only way Agatha can touch you, honey, is through me," he said gruffly. "In the past few weeks I've found myself in the unique position of being at the root of most of your unhappiness. I'd give anything if we could go back a few months, back to the easy way we once lived. But that's not possible, is it?"

"No." Shay slowly shook her head, her emotional state at an all-time low. "It's not possible."

"You really don't love me, you know," he told her, reaching for her hand lying between them on the seat and squeezing it tightly in his own large one. "I'm a fixture in your life, Shay, nothing more."

"Perhaps you're right," she said in an emotionless voice, "perhaps you're right."

The remainder of the drive was made in silence. Kurt was cursing himself for ever having allowed his control to slip, thereby casting their relationship onto an entirely different level. Shay was attempting to accept that a part of her—the portion of her life she'd always associated with Kurt—was gone forever.

When they reached Kurt's house, Shay was out of the car and beginning her way toward the hedge separating their houses before Kurt's feet swung to the ground. He stood by the car, stifling his initial urge to call after her or even follow her.

Let her go. All his instincts told him it was the decent and honorable thing to do, but deep in his heart Kurt wasn't so convinced.

Just as Shay was about to insert her key into the lock, the front door was opened by Becky Walters.

"Surprise!" she cried as she stepped back, then threw an arm around her roommate's shoulders.

"I'll say." Shay grinned. "I've been looking for you at least a week. What happened? Where on earth have you been?"

"I, um, went to visit my sister."

"You did?" Shay replied in a surprised but happy voice. "Oh, Becky, that's nice. How did it go?"

"Okay. Actually, I enjoyed myself."

"I'm glad." Shay smiled. "Can you use a cup of tea?" she called out as she went into her bedroom and stepped out of the high heels. She unzipped the yellow dress, then pushed it down over her hips and stepped out of it.

"The kettle's already on," Becky informed her as they continued the conversation. "Where have you been?"

"Dinner with Agatha."

"Oh, no!" She shook her dark-brown head.

"Actually," Shay said, grinning while she pulled on silky blue pajamas, "it wasn't so bad. After her first blatant remarks regarding how suitable Kurt and I were for each other, she 'almost' behaved herself."

"Well," Becky muttered dryly as she poured steaming hot water into two separate mugs, "having to be around that old biddy, whether she's behaving or not, is enough to give me the shudders."

Shay walked into the kitchen, buttoning her pajama top on the way. "I kind of admire her, myself."

"Why?" Becky asked disbelievingly.

Shay shrugged. "She's old, but she's fighting to retain her independence and trying desperately to keep some semblance of a grip on her life as she's always known it. In spite of Agatha's sharp tongue, I find that touching."

"That's because you're a sap where old folks, animals, and children are concerned. How is our sexy neighbor? I assume you were with him this evening?"

"He's fine, and, yes, I was," Shay answered without betraying the aching loneliness at the mention of Kurt's name.

They were sitting down at the table enjoying their tea when Becky shocked Shay by announcing that she was being transferred to her company's international offices in New York.

"That's terrible," Shay murmured sympathetically, knowing how her roommate had been dreading such a thing happening. The few months they'd been living together, Shay had become quite fond of the other girl. "They've kept you here as a courier only seven months; perhaps the time in the Big Apple will be even less."

"One can only hope," Becky murmured resignedly. "And the kicker is, I have to be there in two weeks."

"Oh, no!" Shay exclaimed. "What with you still having to go here and there, that barely

93

gives you time enough to pack, not to mention a party or anything."

"No parties, please," Becky begged. "I've gotten attached to quite a number of people here. I'm afraid good-bye isn't going to be easy as it is."

Later, as Shay lay in bed, staring into the dark, she wondered how she would cope with the lonely days ahead. Her relationship with Kurt was over, and now she would be losing a friend when Becky moved. It seemed as if everything was happening to her at once, and she didn't like it.

Nicholas Pappolas sat at the massive desk that dominated his large New York office, his dark gaze carefully going over each word of the report he'd received that morning from Ian Deaton. For the first time in ages hope was stirring in his heart. As he read on, Nicholas saw that the detective had been forced to overcome some very substantial odds in gleaning his information.

Ian wrote that a woman by the name of Marie Connors, who had been a close friend of Emily's, had died eleven months ago. He also related another interesting incident. Approximately four weeks after her death another detective had been in town, asking questions regarding Marie Connors and Emily Crawford. Apparently every lead Ian uncovered found him following in the wake of the other detective.

After a moment of casual reflection Nicholas remembered having heard Emily mention someone by the name of Marie. In fact, wasn't Marie the name of the woman who had stayed with Emily's husband, thus enabling Emily to get away occasionally? Nicholas read on, pleased with what had been accomplished so far. Apparently the detective had been forced to go through years and years of old records in the county courthouse in order to find pertinent information regarding Emily and her family as well as the accident. From there he'd had to trace references to a trust fund set up for Emily's minor child. It was the trust fund, Ian wrote, that he was hoping would give him the break he needed. Deaton might be getting on in years, Nicholas mused, but he was doing a damn fine job.

He read again Ian's slanted scrawl in a personal note, inquiring as to whether or not he was to continue. In the note Ian was diligent in carrying out his duty, reminding Nicholas of the possible repercussions for a great many people.

For a moment Nicholas paused, lifting his eyes to stare out the window. In his haste to finally get some sort of investigative action going, he'd forgotten that he wasn't the only one involved. He didn't want to hurt anyone, but he simply had to know if he had a child.

From the moment he'd hired Ian Deaton, he'd been at peace. He felt as if he had a mission in life. It was almost as if—one way or the other—he would be free of the past that had haunted him for years. Oh, yes, he definitely wanted the detective to continue.

CHAPTER FIVE

The doorbell sounded promptly at seven-thirty. Shay scooped up her small clutch and wrap, then hurried from her bedroom.

When she opened the door, Wes Pollock was standing with one shoulder against the wall, a finger about to sound the bell again.

"Don't be so impatient," Shay said sternly, though her tone was belied by the dancing light in her eyes. "It would have served you right if I'd been thirty minutes or so late." Her brown gaze ran appreciatively over him. Wes was a handsome man with dark hair and laughing green eyes. He was of medium height, had a good build, and was one of Shay's closest friends.

"I can't be patient when I'm about to spend an evening with you. I can't wait for the rapture to begin," Wes intoned solemnly, his lips suspiciously twitching.

"That is quite possibly the biggest crock of the year," Shay said disgustedly. "Frankly, knowing you as long as I have, I would've sworn you could do better."

"It's an off night." Wes shrugged good-naturedly. He held the navy-blue velvet cape and placed it on her shoulders, humming off key as he did so. His hand was firm beneath her elbow as they walked the short distance to his car.

As he reached around her and opened the door, Shay heard the distinctive sound of Kurt's Mercedes not twenty feet away in the next yard. When the slamming of the car door came, Shay glanced toward the hedges in spite of constantly arguing with herself not to do so.

It was as if Kurt had personally engineered that brief meeting of their eyes. He neither smiled nor frowned, and Shay felt a sick feeling in the pit of her stomach as she stared at the emotionless mask. Even his eyes, eyes that she'd always been able to read without difficulty, seemed bent on keeping their secrets hidden from her. They swept over her from head to toe, but they revealed nothing.

At his barely perceptible nod Shay responded in kind, then turned her attention back to the unsuspecting Wes. The entire sequence of events had taken only seconds, but to Shay, time had stretched endlessly as she'd gazed into the depths of Kurt's dark-brown eyes.

She settled back in the seat, outwardly calm and poised. Inwardly she felt unsettled. Not only was she missing not being a part of Kurt's life, she missed his barging into her house and *her* life. It was as if a vital part of her was missing and she hadn't the slightest idea how to recover it.

Kurt snatched up his briefcase and strode angrily into the house. "Damn it all!" he exclaimed in a savage voice. Once inside he went directly to the cabinet where the liquor was kept and poured himself a straight Scotch.

After downing the drink and finding that his perspective where Shay was concerned hadn't altered significantly, he removed his jacket and tie and had a second Scotch.

His mind was taken over with continuous pictures of Shay in the arms of Wes Pollock . . . of Wes making love to her . . . of them dancing and then making love . . . of them laughing and talking and then making love. On and on the torturous carousel of images tormented him as they played a naughty game of hide-and-seek through his mind.

It had been four days since dinner at Agatha's, Kurt thought bitterly. Four lousy, stinking days during which he'd heaped all sorts of mental abuse upon his head. Still he was no closer to untangling the snarled ends of the inexplicable bond that existed between Shay and himself, nor the seemingly insoluble tension that had arisen in the relationship. He didn't like it, he told himself . . . didn't like it at all.

When dinner was ended, Shay and Wes joined friends at another club for dancing. By nine-thirty, however, Shay knew the dancing was a mistake. Her head ached, and she was almost out on her feet. This was the fourth night in a row she'd been out, and it was telling on her.

"What happened to the brilliant conversationalist at dinner?" Wes remarked teasingly as they made their way back to their table. "I get the feeling that if you were to stand still longer than five minutes you would be asleep."

"It's simple, really." Shay chuckled in spite of her weariness. "If I were to stand still for *three* minutes I would go to sleep."

"Why so tired? A long day at work?"

"No. Four consecutive nights out."

"Hmmm," Wes murmured consideringly. "I must be getting senile. For the life of me I can't remember us going out since Saturday night."

"We didn't," Shay answered with a grin, "but Max and I went to dinner on Sunday evening, and Roger and I went to dinner and a movie on Monday evening."

"I'm crushed that you would dare mention those other names in my presence," Wes remarked in a comically subdued tone. "How can you even consider going out with a Max or a Roger, when you can have me?"

"Believe me, it's a difficult decision, but I feel I must to take my mind off you!"

"Let's go to my place."

"Why?"

"So we can make love . . . of course," he told her without the slightest variation in his voice. "If you'd only follow my suggestions once, I'm sure it would be a foregone conclusion afterward that I'm the greatest lover in the world."

"You're too modest," Shay managed with a straight face.

"And your answer?"

"Er . . . may I please have a rain check?" she continued the charade.

"Certainly. But I feel I must warn you. That has been your answer the last fifty times I've propositioned you."

"How thoughtless of me. I'll try to do better in the future. On the other hand," she added with a wicked grin, "you could say there's a message in my stock answer."

"I refuse to accept whatever it is your stock answer implies." Wes grinned. "Haven't you yet discovered that I'm the eternal optimist? If I ask you often enough, you might forget one day and say yes."

"You do realize, don't you, that you are quite probably mentally ill?"

"Because I keep trying to get you in my bed? Or because I chase women in general?" He laughed, not embarrassed in the slightest.

"Yes."

"But that's my mission on this earth. Just think how dreary the lives of the women I know would be if I were to be suddenly whisked from their midst." He shook his head, an expression of mock sadness covering his face. "I can't bear to think of the bitter disappointments."

"Whose disappointments?" Hal Dempsey asked, as he and his date reached the table. He shot Shay a knowing grin. "You really shouldn't be seen with that guy, you know. He has a terrible reputation."

That remark set off a round of humorous and insulting exchanges between the guys that lasted till the two couples separated in the parking lot an hour and a half later. There was such a comfortable silence in the car during the drive to her house, Shay found herself on the point of dozing a couple of times. She tried to cover it up, but with the last nod drew an amused chuckle from Wes.

"You do realize that you've done irreparable damage to my self-esteem, don't you? You're the first woman I've ever been out with who's fallen asleep on the way home."

"Mark it up to exhaustion and not the company," Shay quipped, not at all apologetic.

"That's even worse." He scowled. "You became exhausted by staying out with other men." He cocked his head and sighed. "I'm not sure I can recover from such a severe put-down."

At Shay's front door Wes gave her no cause to evade his kiss. "I refuse to kiss someone who gives the impression of being in a coma . . . even a very beautiful coma." He touched his lips to her forehead and stepped back. "Becoming friends with you was a mistake." He glared at her, though nothing could hide the amusement in his eyes. "It's given me a conscience. I should have kept our relationship on a more . . . sophisticated plane."

"You're really a very nice man," she told him, laughing, "in spite of trying hard not to be. Good night, Wes."

"Good night. I'll call you in a couple of days."

Shay stepped inside and closed the door, a huge yawn almost splitting her face.

"Sounds like a great evening!" Becky grinned, choosing that exact same moment to enter the living room from the kitchen. "Was Wes that boring?"

"Robert Redford couldn't have kept me awake this evening. I almost fell asleep while eating dinner, while dancing, and during the drive home. Even knowing Wes as well as I do, I'm embarrassed."

"Feel awake enough to have a quick cup of tea?"

"Sure," Shay agreed. Actually, she didn't, but there wouldn't be many more opportunities for her and Becky to have one of their late-night talks. "I'll miss this," she said, trailing Becky into the kitchen, then sitting down at the table.

Becky grimaced. "I've come to realize that making and leaving close friends is one of the drawbacks of this courier job."

"Well, don't worry. We'll have to see what we can do with vacations," Shay suggested. "Since the airlines are always competing with each other, the fares from one coast to the other are much more reasonable."

After a little while they both said good-night. Shay went through her nightly ritual of teeth brushing, face cleaning, and getting into her pajamas in a comical zombielike state.

The only jarring note came when she hesitated by the window before slipping into bed. She drew open the draperies, as was her nightly habit once the lamp was off, and stared toward the Barron house. Her gaze became pinned on the darkened double windows of Kurt's bedroom. She saw that the sliding glass doors he'd had installed during one of his and Agatha's "periods of renovation" were open.

Shay's hands gripped the edge of the window till her knuckles showed white. That meant he wasn't resting any better than she. At least she hoped it did. She leaned forward, straining her eyes for a glimpse of him. Old habits were hard to break, and she knew for a fact that when Kurt was worried or had something important on his mind, he became an insomniac and took long walks at night. Before their recent "estrangement" Shay knew she wouldn't have hesitated even a second before joining him. But not now.

What was it he'd said to her? "It's only infatuation that you feel for me. Wait six months." Hopefully within six months, Kurt would have moved, and she would be in Europe. She sighed.

But at the moment he was out enjoying a leisurely stroll. "Lucky him," she muttered in disgust. "He's a man, and can get by with wandering around till all hours." A brief grin hovered over her lips as a sudden burst of inspiration struck her. "I should sneak out and hide behind a bush. When Mr. Barron strolls by, I should then knock the flaming hell out of him with a baseball bat!"

With that satisfying thought lending her a measure of contentment, she climbed into bed and pulled the covers up to her chin. It wasn't fair, she thought as she yawned, wallowing in self-pity. She was exhausted, forced to go out each evening in order not to scream, or even worse, bang her head against a wall, and it was all Kurt's fault. All Kurt's fault . . . she remembered faintly as she drifted off to sleep . . . all Kurt's fault. . . .

But in that same sleep Shay continually found herself facing a scowling Kurt, rubbing his head—where a tremendous bump was visible—and yelling at her, while she brandished her baseball bat like a machete.

The next morning, just as Shay was pouring herself her first cup of coffee, the phone rang.

"Miss Michaels?" a woman's voice purred— there was no other word for it, Shay thought— in her ear.

"Yes."

"This is Colleen Gray. I'm Kurt Barron's 'private secretary.' " She emphasized the last two words in a manner that had Shay gritting her teeth. Why was it that most women over the age of ten were in awe of the infernal man? And just who the hell was this Colleen woman anyway? And where on earth did Kurt find female employees with such seductive voices? Better still, where was reliable, steady Miss Stokes, who had worked for Kurt for over twelve years, and who treated Shay like a member of her family? "The plants in the reception area are beginning to look bedraggled. I'm sure, since this is your bread and butter," she twittered, "you want to make sure your little darlings always look their best. Is there any chance you could change them today?"

"Change them?" Shay repeated. Was the damn woman crazy? Did she have any idea at all what it meant to change such a display? "All of them?" It had only been a few days since she'd watered and fertilized all Kurt's plants, and they'd looked super then. They weren't due a complete rotation for another three months. She couldn't begin to imagine what the problem could be. "Exactly what do you mean by bedraggled?"

"Wilted," the overly gracious Miss Gray solemnly announced.

"Wilted?" Shay repeated like a parrot.

"Quite dreadfully, I'm afraid. Mr. Barron was just in here and remarked that something would definitely have to be done."

"Oh, he did, did he?" Shay came near to snarling. "Please tell *Mr. Barron* that I will take care of the problem immediately. Er . . . is Miss Stokes on vacation?"

"I'm sorry, Miss Michaels, but I don't discuss personnel problems with strangers."

Ooooh! Shay silently groaned. At that precise moment nothing would have suited her better than to have her hands around the faceless woman's throat! She slammed down the receiver, her cheeks red with anger. Stranger indeed!

Some forty-five minutes later a flinty-eyed Shay stood in Kurt's reception room, staring disbelievingly at the mass of wilted greenery.

107

The lovely spathaphylum, one of her favorites, was beyond help. Three huge ferns, their fronds reaching in the neighborhood of five feet or better, were a sickly shade of blue. The other plants were in varying degrees of deterioration.

Suddenly, as she struggled to find some plausible explanation for the travesty before her, Shay realized she was beginning to perspire. She glanced toward the receptionist's desk where, at the moment, no one was sitting, and wondered what the devil was going on. Was it really as warm as she was feeling or was it—in her case—a simple case of nerves? After all, she reasoned, there was the distinct possibility she would be running into Kurt.

"Isn't that a sad-looking sight?"

Shay whirled around to find Kurt standing in the doorway of the conference room. He wasn't wearing a jacket, and his tie was loosened as if he'd been working intently. The sleeves of his white shirt were turned back, revealing the thickness of his tanned forearms, and the dark hair that grew there. His gorgeous brown eyes and his sensuous mouth were too seductive. He looked fantastic, Shay thought with an inwardly sigh, and that fact alone irritated the hell out of her. She wanted him to give the appearance of death warmed over!

"I can't remember ever seeing anything

worse." She turned back to the wilted plants, hating that she'd seen him, but glad as well. These peculiar feelings she'd begun having for Kurt were about to get the best of her, she worried. Never in her entire life had she been a wishy-washy sort of person. Now, suddenly, she couldn't think a simple thought through without changing her silly mind five or six times. There'd been moments in the past few weeks when she'd honestly wondered if she were losing her grip on reality. "Any inkling as to what happened?"

"None."

Kurt couldn't tear his eyes away from Shay. Part of him wanted to roar with laughter at the expression on her adorable face when he'd caught her unawares as she'd been studying her plants.

He shrugged one broad shoulder. There'd be hell to pay later, if she ever found out what had really happened. He'd hated harming her plants, but it was about the only way he knew of getting her in the office other than on the visits she made regarding the routine care of the plants. And she was avoiding him on those visits.

Too many days had gone by with his catching only brief glimpses of her. And last night was just too much! Kurt remembered the surge of absolute rage that had exploded inside him when he saw her going out with Wes Pollock. His reaction had shocked him.

Wes wasn't a bad guy, Kurt had consoled himself as he surreptitiously watched them walk toward the car. He was closer to Shay's age, and they seemed to have a lot in common. But when Shay looked up and met Kurt's gaze, he realized then that Wes's character or that of anyone she dated mattered little to him. They could have patterned their lives after the pope and it would have been the same. It boiled down to one simple thing: He was jealous as hell.

Shay bent down to part the wilted fronds and branches of greenery so that she could better observe the soil. Perhaps some kind of parasite had attacked the root systems. But as she remained leaning over, with one hand clutching a goodly amount of black soil, a peculiar yet familiar aroma hit her.

Bourbon?

She stared at the dirt in her hand, then back at the long planter. Of course not. She smiled rather sardonically, feeling quite foolish at the ridiculous flight of fancy her thoughts had taken. Nobody in his right mind would pour bourbon or Scotch or any type of alcoholic beverage on an expensive planter such as this one. Why, that would be terrible.

Shay dropped the dirt, brushed her palms together, then turned to the carryall she'd brought in with her and began removing several small jars in which to put soil samples. "I'll send these to the lab," she spoke over her shoulder to Kurt, who was still watching her. "In the meantime I'll get started on having all this and the soil removed"—she waved one slim hand toward the mass of greenery—"then replant."

"What a huge job," Kurt said with feigned concern.

"I'll manage," Shay replied, watching his approach with an expression akin to pure, unadulterated panic. What on earth was there about him lately to seriously affect her breathing, her ability to reason and to stand? It didn't used to be that way.

When he was only a foot or two away, Kurt stopped. Without being able to control it, he extended his hand to brush lightly back from her forehead a lock of softly curling hair. He wanted to touch her—and if he were to follow the honest dictates of his heart, he told himself, he would take her in his arms and hold her.

Instead he placed his wrist on her shoulder, letting his hand hang behind her. It was, he reasoned, as if he were bent on punishing himself by touching Shay impersonally rather than possessively, roughly, as a lover might in a moment of passion. "Let the plants wait for a while. Let's go to my office and have something to drink."

Shay was tempted to say no. Unequivocally . . . no! But the scent of him and the unholy pleasure of being close to him was her undoing. "All right," she said softly, allowing him to turn her and gently push her forward. "I could almost swear someone has poured at least a gallon of bourbon into your planter," she said casually as they entered the room that served as his home-away-from-home. At least the subject of his withered plants would give them something safe to discuss. Shay dropped down onto one of the long sofas and feasted her eyes on his every move.

"You're kidding," Kurt spoke over his shoulder. He turned then, his features a mask of polite curiosity. "What would you like to drink, Miss Michaels?" he asked, grinning as he remembered the last time he'd offered her something without first asking her preference.

"Do you have orange juice?"

"Orange juice coming right up. Getting back to the plants. I can't imagine why anyone would want to pour good bourbon on plants, can you?"

Shay opened her mouth to give him a sharp put-down, but as he turned and walked toward her, she saw the teasing glint in his dark eyes. Damn him! He was changing the rules again. "Why indeed?" She sighed defeatedly. She took the tall, frosty glass of juice, bracing herself emotionally when he dropped down beside her. "Although if I were you, I'd sure as the devil find out. The large plants you had out there don't come cheap."

Suddenly she could feel her arms prickling with goose pimples—and for once she was positive it wasn't from Kurt's close proximity. She frowned. "You have the craziest air-conditioning system in this office I've ever been exposed to. I was perspiring like mad out there"—she nodded behind her toward the reception area —"and in here I'm freezing to death. You should have it checked."

"Perhaps you're coming down with something," Kurt replied silkily. "You've been leading such an active social life lately, I'm surprised you can even get out of bed in the mornings."

Shay wanted to lash out at him, wanted to bombard him with awful hurting words, but she didn't. Her pride wouldn't let her. Instead, she allowed her head to relax against the stuffed back of the sofa and gave him the perfect facsimile of a contented smile. "Oh, well, you know how it is, Kurt, when you're having fun. . . ."

When the tiny muscle in his cheek began to thump like crazy, it was all Shay could do to keep from laughing. "Who are you seeing these days? I'm sure the ever-persistent Tessa is in there pitching for her share of your attention, but who else have you added to your stable of women since we last talked?"

"At least five," Kurt answered without a moment's hesitation. He'd been damned near killing himself with work for the last week or so, but he sure as hell wasn't going to admit that to the blue-eyed minx seated next to him. Her very nearness was like some dangerous bomb exploding in his veins. His nerves were taut to the point of snapping. She was tying him in knots without the slightest effort on her part.

But why? he kept asking himself. Why?

He'd known Shay practically all her life. Why had she suddenly become such an unsettling force now? Why was he finding himself wanting to murder the men she dated? Why was he having practically to tie himself in his house in the evenings to keep from running over to her place and spending every possible minute with her? And worst of all (he silently groaned) why on earth had he been so stupid as to have brought sex into their relationship that day when he'd found her asleep in the tub?

In his mind he could still feel the weight of her small, perfect breast in his palm, and the silkiness of her skin against his fingertips.

"Are you going to Margetta Boyd's party this evening?" Shay asked in an effort to break the tense silence. This was Kurt, she kept telling herself. The same Kurt she'd never stood on ceremony with before, the same Kurt she'd felt as relaxed and free with as a brother. But no matter how hard she tried to convince herself into believing that, it didn't work. In her heart Shay was forced to accept that the Kurt of her past was lost to her forever. But the Kurt of the future? . . . now, that was an entirely different story, she mused, a gleam of mischief in her eyes.

CHAPTER SIX

When there was no response to her question, Shay turned her curly brown head and stared at Kurt, who seemed lost in thought. The tiny, devilish imp lounging on her shoulder urged her on.

"Are you ignoring me, Kurt?" she asked softly. As she spoke, Shay moved closer to him, bringing her jean-clad thigh to rest against his firm one.

Kurt's head swiveled around as if he'd been zapped, his brown eyes boring into her blue ones before dropping to the rather intimate position of their thighs.

"Wha—what did you say?" he muttered hoarsely. He took her glass, then leaned forward and set both glasses of juice on the table in front of the sofa. He leaned back, his movements cautious. It was as if he was expecting trouble any second.

Shay turned toward him then, drawing her ankles beneath her. This new adjustment in her position had her not only with her thighs resting on his, but with an arm casually draped across his shoulder. "I said"—she smiled warmly—"are you ignoring me?" Before he could answer, she allowed her fingers to caress idly the turn of his ear . . . then move on to find amusement by touching and smoothing the edges of his hair just above his collar.

Kurt sat like a stone! "No. What else did you ask me?" he asked in a voice closely resembling a croak.

"I can't remember."

Shay was finding it almost impossible not to burst out laughing at him. Yet at the same time she wanted to strangle him for his stubbornness. A determined gleam appeared in her eyes. She liked a challenge as much as he did, she decided. Besides, if for the past few weeks he hadn't been acting like a cold fish, she wouldn't have minded so much. But he had been, she reasoned, and she did, and he was about to be introduced to her "Seduction by Shay" routine. Succeeding chapters would follow as needed.

"Your hair is so nice and thick," she murmured, moving even closer to him so that her lips were touching his ear. "It's amazing. I've known you forever and I've touched you, yet at this moment I feel as if I've really never 'touched' you. Do you understand?" When he remained as responsive as a rock in a coma, she

117

went on. "Sometimes I wake up in the middle of the night and find myself wondering what it would be like to run my fingers through this gorgeous hair . . . like this," she added as her fingers buried themselves in the dark growth.

"What the hell are you doing, Shay?" Kurt demanded. One large hand reached up and captured her wrist and dragged it away from its deliberate teasing. He was positive that at any second he was going into orbit! His body was experiencing the strangest extremes. How was it possible for a person to be ice-cold and hot as fire at the same time? If he wasn't careful, he cautioned himself, he would have this blue-eyed witch in his bed before she could blink her eyes. Damn! She was as potent as one-hundred-proof bourbon and just as lethal.

First thing after lunch, he promised himself irrationally, he was going to put his place up for sale. There was no way he could continue to live next door to a female as aggravating . . . as sexy . . . as irritating . . . as lovely . . . oh, hell! His breath came out in a powerful whoosh! Judas priest! He'd never faced such a stacked deck in his life.

"Why, Kurt daarling," Shay replied with feigned innocence. Her head dipped to an engaging angle and her lips curved into the perfect pout. "I haven't the faintest idea what you're talking about."

Kurt stared hard at her, the heat of his gaze

almost causing Shay to drop her head in embarrassment. "You're acting like a woman on the make," he said bluntly. "And it doesn't suit you."

"Maybe I am," she retorted in an outwardly calm voice. "And if you find me lacking in polish, then be patient. In a few weeks I'll be able to compete with the best of them."

Kurt briefly closed his eyes, his lips compressed into a straight, rigid line. With each thump of his heart the tiny muscle in his cheek was beating so rapidly, Shay was positive it would leap through his skin. She tried to disengage her wrist from his hand, but his hold only tightened. That was strange, she mused, then just as quickly realized that it wasn't strange at all. In fact, it was precisely in keeping with the erratic way Kurt had been behaving for weeks now. At the moment, however, she could see that he was having a difficult time controlling his emotions. It was also obvious that he was quite definitely aroused in another way.

Well, at least he wasn't totally unaware of her, Shay thought, embarrassed and at the same time relieved. Though she wouldn't be at all surprised if he were to deny completely what was so obvious to her, and try to make her believe she was hallucinating.

"Tell me the name of the man you and I discussed that afternoon in your greenhouse, Shay," Kurt requested in measured tones. "You remember," he continued doggedly, "he was the one you were considering having an affair with. You wanted my advice on whether or not to let him know how you feel. I advised you against doing such a thing. How's that relationship coming along?"

Shay stared at him for several seconds, then looked past his shoulder, her chin unconsciously lifting a fraction of an inch. "It's—coming," she hedged. "Why do you ask?"

"Because I don't believe there is another man. Or rather," he quickly corrected, "I think I'm the man to whom you were alluding."

"Oh? And exactly when did you become a psychic?"

"It's really quite simple," he answered, forcing himself to keep his tone as impersonal as possible. "You wouldn't be coming on to me the way you have been, honey, if there was another man in your life who you were serious about." His thumb was gently caressing the quivering pulse in her wrist, and it was all he could do to keep from raising the tender spot to his lips. Every nerve ending in his body was crying out for the touch of her, for the feel of her soft body against his. "I'm flattered as hell, honey, but it can't be."

In light of such a preponderance of evidence against her, she had little choice but to be annoyingly candid. "So?" she quipped with an arrogant toss of her head. "Sue me."

"I think what you need, young lady, is a good spanking," he said sternly.

Shay favored him with a look so full of disgust, Kurt couldn't help but grin. "Please . . . don't you think you've overdone the big-brother routine just a bit? I'm twenty-three years old now, Kurt, not three." She went on distinctly and slowly, "I'm an adult, for Pete's sake! Treat me like one."

"I can't stop caring and fussing over you. You're as much a part of my life as the air I breathe, Shay. I suppose that's one reason I can't suddenly switch roles in the middle of the stream." Kurt continued. "For years I've felt responsible for you. Even when I wasn't here, I thought about you. We've shared so much, honey. I can't let that go, nor can I abruptly switch roles and whisk you into my bed and make love to you." He shook his head and exhaled sharply. "This new position you've suddenly elevated me to is giving me some bad moments."

Shay regarded him for a moment, then slumped back against the sofa. Damn! He was without a doubt the most irritating human being on earth! "You would like for me to ignore what I feel for you?" she said tightly. "Even though at the moment I'm not sure what it is," she added honestly. "And would you also like for me to ignore what I know you . . . feel for me?" she asked pointedly, easing the calf of her

121

leg lightly over that part of him which was so blatantly willing to do her bidding.

"Precisely," Kurt snapped. He pushed her abruptly off his lap and rose to his feet. He walked over and stared out the wide wraparound expanse of glass that graced most of his personal offices. "I think you'd better go, Shay," he threw over his shoulder. His voice was cold, not at all in keeping with the temperature of his body, he thought angrily.

In the background he could hear the slight rustle of fabric as Shay got to her feet. From there he followed her—in his mind's eye—to the door, through his private office, and back to her miniature forest of wilted greenery.

When he was sure he was alone, Kurt turned and stared unseeingly at the room before him. He could not get Shay's face out of his head. He'd confronted all sorts of problems in his career. There'd been long, tough fights in the boardroom, just as there'd been numerous struggles and battles in his climb to the powerful position he was in today. But he knew that never in his life could he recall a situation such as he found himself in at the moment.

It was a case of trying to do the honorable thing regarding someone he cared about, and having that same someone almost hate him for it. Shay was known for her impulsiveness, and now all her determination and attention were directed toward him. Kurt wondered just how long he would remain the loyal "friend" he'd always been.

Suddenly Shay appeared in the doorway. Kurt stared darkly at her.

"You never did give me an answer," she remarked as if nothing at all had happened between them.

"An answer to what?"

"Are you going to Margetta Boyd's party this evening?"

"Are you?"

"Not if it will make you uneasy," Shay said softly.

"I suppose you're so busy you can pick and choose, hmmmm?" Kurt murmured harshly.

Shay shrugged. "Something like that. But just remember, we're going to run into each other from time to time. Will you be able to handle it?"

Christ, this was a switch! Here was a relative innocent asking him, who had discarded the women in his life as easily as he'd done with his shirts, if he could handle a situation involving her "puppy love" for him.

"I'll handle it."

"Great. See ya later."

Phillip Norcross locked the door of his private office—located in a New York skyscraper whose first seven floors served as office space for Pappolas Shipping—then walked purposefully to his desk and seated himself. After selecting a small key from a gold ring, he opened a drawer and removed a manila folder. He leaned back, his shrewd, dark eyes running over the information that had been so costly . . . so shocking.

He also reread the letter. A letter that could appear so innocent to anyone catching a glimpse of it . . . or even reading it. But later, when he'd met and had dinner with the writer of said missive, the innocent rhetoric had become separate and individual words of damnation. The person responsible for the awakening had overwhelming proof. Nicholas Pappolas had an heir, a child he knew nothing about. And he, Phillip, if he were to step into the role of leadership he'd envisioned for himself, would have to see that his uncle never knew of his real child.

Each time Phillip reviewed the folder, he could feel the anger rebuilding in him, and the almost uncontrollable urge to destroy rippling throughout his body.

He, and only he, would be Nicholas's heir.

Phillip looked up from the report and stared thoughtfully into space, remembering how he'd hired the best detective money could buy to investigate the information that had been given to him. He also remembered the sense of disbelief he'd experienced when the detective had corroborated the informant's story.

124

That had been a number of months back. Months during which Phillip had, as he was still having, problems deciding how best to handle the informant, not to mention the actual heir to the Pappolas shipping fortune. Two unwanted people making their presence felt in his life.

He reached for the phone and dialed. When a voice answered, Phillip was brief and to the point. "I think it's time for us to get together and compare notes."

"I'll be in New York on Thursday. Lunch or dinner?"

"Call me when you arrive and I'll let you know."

Phillip replaced the receiver, a quiver of distaste visible at the side of his mouth. He didn't like being forced to deal with a blackmailer. And that's precisely what he considered the person he'd just spoken with. At the moment Phillip felt he was in command . . . but only just. By the same token, at any given moment the blackmailer could contact Nicholas. Phillip had to be certain that didn't happen—no matter what was necessary to ensure such silence.

Shay could feel tiny beads of perspiration forming on her forehead as she whirled and swayed provocatively to the beat of the fast rock number. The music had kept Margetta Boyd's guests in good spirits; few of them had sat out more than one number at a time. It was a great party, and Shay was having a good time . . . for the most part.

That part that kept it from being a perfect evening was Kurt. Ahhh, yes, Kurt, she thought roughly. He'd made his appearance less than an hour ago, with a sultry redhead on his arm. Shay was still smarting from the cold, almost angry glare with which he'd regarded her when she'd danced by him. His dark gaze had slammed into the provocative V-neckline of her red dress. She'd deliberately turned away from the fierceness of his inspection, and impudently presented him the other view of her dress . . . the halter top leaving her back bare from neck to waist.

Since that impromptu meeting—if it could actually be called such—she had gone to great pains to avoid any further confrontations with her neighbor till later in the evening when she knew she would have consumed enough champagne to make her brain fuzzy. That way, she reasoned, she could easily credit whatever act of misconduct she was likely to commit (for there would be no way of getting through the evening without Kurt's being displeased with her) to her being slightly inebriated.

Even though Kurt was going to be there, Shay had no intention of staying away from the party. Aside from the fact that Margetta was her friend as well as Jane's, Shay had also arranged the flowers for the occasion. The Boyds were as wealthy as Kurt, and the home Margetta and her husband shared with his parents was absolutely huge. Shay had felt drained when she'd finished the flowers a scant two hours before the party began.

"Looking over the competition?" a gyrating Ted Corley asked breathlessly in front of Shay. His blond hair was mussed, and he looked like a kid instead of a successful thirty-four-year-old dentist.

She looked at her tall, lanky brother-in-law and smiled. "How did you guess?" She grinned easily, her own breathing rather erratic as well. Ted was a darling, and Shay adored him. "Do you have any idea what my sister is doing while you're acting like a fifteen-year-old?"

"She's over there with our hostess, helping to fund-raise." He nodded toward the other side of the room where Jane, Margetta, and Kurt were talking. "Looks like Margetta will get that new wing for her building after all, doesn't it? I'm sure that before this evening's over, she'll have in hand personal donations from Kurt and most of the wealthier guests present."

"She really does know how to get blood out of the proverbial turnip," Shay quipped. "But I must admit all her projects are worthwhile ones. This latest one will really benefit the elderly."

"I'm sure it will," Ted murmured. "Kurt seems to be looking tired these days." He grinned. "Must be exhausting living the life of the total bachelor." He gave Shay a sideways glance, then pretended an inordinate interest in his observation of Kurt. Ted had often remarked to Jane that he was positive Shay was in love with Kurt Barron, and wondered when his sister-in-law would realize that small fact.

"I wouldn't know. I don't keep track of his life-style." Shay answered hautily.

"Of course not." Ted laughed. The number ended and they made their way back to the small table just as Jane arrived with Kurt. "Glad you came over, old buddy." Ted thumped Kurt on the back. "Two women in one evening are more than I can handle. On the other hand, I was just telling Shay here that you look like you've been partying too much." He leaned close and whispered conspiratorially. "Why don't you let me fill in for you for a few days? You look about ready to drop."

"Thanks, Ted." Kurt grinned. "You're all heart." His gaze shifted to Shay, who was deliberately ignoring him by pretending to watch the people at the next table. Immediately he masked his face in a scowl. God! Wasn't she aware that he, or anyone else for that matter, could see a good portion of her breasts . . . and what they couldn't see left little to the imagination? What the hell was wrong with

Ted and Jane? Did they want Shay flaunting her—her femininity in front of the whole world? Without stopping to consider his actions, he stepped the few steps around the table, then reached down and caught Shay's wrist.

"Let's dance."

"How kind of you to ask," she began the moment she recognized the voice. That was at the same moment she felt herself being hoisted from the chair as if a forklift had attached its powerful force to her body. "But I really don't care to dance with you," she said icily to the broad back behind which she was being towed like a tugboat.

"Shut up!" Kurt angrily snapped the moment they reached the center of the dance floor. "I should think anyone dressed as you are would welcome another chance to let the other guests see you. You're practically naked." He jerked her into his arms and brought her up roughly against his broad chest.

"You despicable toad!" she hissed. Her blue eyes were glowing with anger, and she was literally standing on her tiptoes in order to be heard over the noise of the band, but not the entire assemblage of guests. "How dare you pass judgment on me like some narrow-minded, evil-thinking, self-righteous ass!"

"Me—pass judgment?" he scoffed scornfully. "That's the laugh of the year. The way you're dressed, every man here has 'passed judgment' on you. And why not? You're on view from your head to your navel in front and from your neck to your behind in back."

Shay was speechless! She tried to wiggle out of his arms, but they merely tightened till her clenched fists were trapped between them, and her nose was buried in his tie. "Let me go," she demanded through clenched teeth.

"No way. You've danced every dance since my arrival, so why not this one with me?"

"Because I happened not to hate the other men I danced with," she remarked savagely, staring straight up into his face. "They were friends and I enjoyed being with them."

"And we definitely aren't friends anymore, are we, Shay?" Kurt said in a peculiar voice.

Suddenly the anger controlling her body abated somewhat, leaving in its course an almost overwhelming urge to cry. "No." She gave a quick, jerky motion with her head. "I suppose we aren't."

Kurt muttered something unintelligible under his breath and pulled her close again. They finished out the dance without another word being spoken between them. When they returned to Shay's table, Kurt stared deep into her eyes, the conflict going on inside him leaving his features cold and stormy. After an electric moment of brutal scrutiny he turned on his heel and walked away. Shay watched him join

130

the redhead he'd brought to the party, then silently cursed herself for the wetness in her eyes that blurred her vision.

Jane and Ted were across the room talking with a group of their friends, and Shay was grateful for the time alone, time in which she tried to compose herself.

"Would you guys mind terribly if I made an early night of it?" she asked the moment Ted and Jane joined her.

"Tired?" Jane asked sympathetically, ignoring the gleam of interest in her husband's eyes.

"Exhausted," Shay confessed. "I spent almost four hours here this afternoon arranging flowers. Matter of fact, I even dressed here." She got to her feet. "I'll give you a call tomorrow. Okay?"

"Sure thing, honey," Jane said warmly. She kissed Shay on the cheek, then sat down.

"How much have you had to drink?" Ted asked.

"Not as much as I would have liked." Shay shrugged. "I'm not drunk, if that's what you're thinking."

"How much?" he insisted.

"Three glasses of champagne."

"Then I'll drive you home," he informed her.

"That's ridiculous," she began to fuss, only to be told to shut up for the second time that evening.

"It won't take him more than thirty minutes to go and come," Jane argued. "If you were to have a wreck, I'd never forgive myself. Neither would Ted."

"Oh . . ." Ted grinned devilishly. "I don't know, I might." Then he quickly bent his lanky frame in order not to have Shay's small clutch nail him on the side of his obnoxious head.

"That will cost you, brother dear." She giggled as she was led across the room. They teased each other and laughed, till they found Margetta so that Shay could say good-night; then were on their way.

Across the room Kurt watched their departure through narrowed lids, then surprised his attractive date by declaring that he was ready to leave.

"But it's still early yet," she protested.

"So it is," Kurt said indifferently. "Would you rather stay and let someone else take you home?"

"Oh . . . I'm sure you wouldn't like that."

"Quite the contrary." He shrugged. "I wouldn't mind at all."

"Oh." She sighed defeatedly, seeing what she'd hoped would be a profitable relationship ended before it even got started. "In that case, I think I will stay on. See you around."

"Sure." Kurt smiled thinly, then turned and made his way through the crowd.

CHAPTER SEVEN

Instead of going straight to bed when she got home, Shay stepped out of her shoes, then decided she needed another glass of wine. "To lift my spirits," she muttered darkly as she made her way through the house. The only lights on were a lamp in the living room, one in her bedroom, and the hood light over the stove in the kitchen. But Shay didn't bother adding additional brilliance to her surroundings. The shadowy world around her was soothing to her depressed state of mind, she rationalized as she poured wine into a stemmed glass.

With wine in hand she slowly made her way back to the living room, where she switched off the lamp, then sprawled on the sofa, a complete picture of dejection. As her head dropped back against the tiny-flowered chintz, her eyes resumed that same suspicious brightening they'd had at the party. Only this time the brightness overspilled and made tiny iridescent trails down her cheeks.

At that precise moment Shay was convinced she hated Kurt Barron. Her mind and senses became deaf and dumb to all sound and thought unless it was directly related to Kurt. I despise him, she continued silently to berate the man responsible for her unhappiness. He's arrogant, inconsiderate and . . . and . . . ? She searched her mind for further disparaging adjectives with which to describe him, but none came readily to the fore.

What had happened to her life? she asked for the hundredth time. Only a few weeks ago she'd been happy as a lark. Exactly when had the tension that now existed between her and Kurt begin? What had brought it on? An unsteady hand raised the glass to her lips. As the wine slipped down her throat, Shay wondered fleetingly if the rest of her life was to be as dismal as the present.

"They say it isn't wise to drink alone."

Heavens! Shay exclaimed in her mind, she was hallucinating. She could have sworn she'd heard Kurt's voice.

"Why don't I join you?"

Shay froze! This time she knew it wasn't a figment of her imagination.

The fine hair on her nape jumped to attention as she sensed him moving over the thick carpet to stand behind her. When she felt the touch of his hands framing her face and tipping her head back to look at him, she offered no resistance.

There was only enough light to make out the outline of him, yet his face needed no light for Shay to know each tiny crease, each faint line.

"For a big man you are incredibly light footed. I didn't even hear you come in."

"Perhaps I should become a cat burglar," he said in a feeble attempt at humor.

"What are you doing here?" she whispered.

"Damned if I know," Kurt said gruffly.

"That's hard to believe. I thought you always had an excellent reason for doing everything."

He continued to stare down at her, deep in thought, while his thumbs lightly smoothed the corners of her mouth. "I was worried about you," he finally said.

"That's hard to believe. You were very rude earlier."

"So I was," he replied in measured tones. Suddenly he bent toward her, his lips touching hers while his hands slipped unhindered beneath the two pieces of material that served as a bodice to the dress she was wearing.

Shay felt as if she'd been zapped by an incredibly large electrical charge! She couldn't move. It was as if some paralysis had invaded her body. Even when Kurt's tongue began its delightful foray against her lips, she didn't respond.

She was frozen into position.

Though his hands still cupped her breasts, Kurt raised his head enough to look at her. "What's wrong?" he whispered hoarsely.

"I think I'm in a state of shock," she said bluntly.

For a moment he seemed to laugh. At least that's what Shay thought, for she was positive she felt his body shake. That irked her.

"It—it—isn't funny in the least," she stuttered.

"I know." He dropped quick kisses on her eyes, her nose, and her mouth.

"Then why are you laughing at me?"

"I haven't the faintest idea," Kurt confessed. "It just struck me as funny. I plan on making love to you, you know." He ran the two sentences together so quickly, it took Shay a moment or two to figure out what he'd said.

"The last conversation I shared with you on that particular subject, you were quite adamant that we not even so much as shake hands for at least six months," Shay murmured. Ohhh . . . she inhaled deeply, he smelled so good. And the way his hands and lips were touching her had her feeling as if a delicious warmth had settled over her entire body.

"You'll learn, as you grow older, honey, never to make rash statements," Kurt said against her lips. "Open your mouth for me." When she complied with that demand, his tongue slipped inside, startling her with its

136

erotic maneuvers. By the time he withdrew to take the tip of one ear into his mouth and caress it, Shay was like putty in his hands.

Reading her response as easily as he'd always done, Kurt leaned over farther and lifted her into his arms. "If I keep hanging over the back of this damn sofa, I'll have a broken back." He turned and walked quickly to her bedroom.

"Mmmmm . . . that would be a pity," Shay murmured in bemused fashion. Her head was cradled beneath his chin, and her eyes were closed. She was dreaming, she kept telling herself. Dreaming the wildest, most fantastic dream of her entire life. And the only way she could keep the dream real was to keep her eyes closed.

"I can tell you're really choked up about it." His voice rumbled in his chest, the sound quite pleasant to Shay's ear. When he reached the antique mahogany poster bed he set her on her feet, his hands going once again to frame her face. The lamp cast a soft, intimate glow over the entire room, as well as the patchwork quilt serving as a coverlet on the bed.

Soft and pretty kept running through Kurt's mind as he stared at Shay. He could also remember times when this petite and fragile beauty in his arms had cursed like a sailor and proceeded to do battle with him at a moment's notice. On one hand she was his talisman—on the other, she was proving to be his nemesis.

"I refuse to make love to a woman who keeps her eyes closed."

Shay opened first one eye, then the other, as if expecting him to evaporate in a puff of air. "I'm afraid that any moment I'll wake up and find that this is some wild figment of my imagination," she said simply.

"Believe me," he said gruffly, "nothing has ever been more real than the two of us standing here." His hands went to the fastener at the back of her neck and released the two ends of material, its slithery descent slowly baring the pink-tipped perfection of her breasts.

Kurt's breath became a painful fullness within his chest as he finished unclothing each delectable inch of her. When she finally stood naked before him, he knew in that moment that he'd give anything to have her painted just as she was, but he also knew it wasn't possible. He could never stand the thought of another man seeing her this way.

He reached out with one large, slightly trembling, hand and clasped it to the indention of her small waist. "You are so very beautiful to me."

"I'm glad," Shay said shyly. She made as if to touch him, then jerked her hand back.

"Don't do that," he whispered huskily, reaching for her hand and bringing it to rest over his heart. "That's part of it. I want you to touch me just the same as I touch you."

"Your heart is beating so fast, I'm afraid it's going to jump out of your chest." She smiled, surprised by the discovery. "I've known you to be aroused once or twice by me in these past few weeks, but I wasn't aware that you felt the same way I do."

"How do you feel, kitten?" Kurt asked. He bent down till his dark head was at her breasts and his lips gently sucking on a pouting nipple. Shay could feel millions of infinitesimal nerves within her body being stretched to their maximum. A surge of weakness swept over her, causing her to grasp at Kurt's arms for support. "Please," she whispered.

He felt her response and raised his head. He could see the even tips of her teeth biting into her lips as she struggled to cope with the rush of feeling he was creating inside her. "I want this to be the most fantastic night of your life," Kurt said softly, then picked her up and placed her on the bed.

It took only a brief moment or two for Kurt to undress, and during that time Shay made no effort to look away. This was Kurt. Her Kurt . . . His body was as she remembered, having seen him in every abbreviated mode of dress for as long as she could remember. Seeing him totally naked, however, merely confirmed her thoughts where he was concerned. He was perfect.

139

"What's the smile for?" Kurt asked as he dropped down beside her, his gaze alert.

"You look like a Greek god," she told him without the slightest bit of embarrassment. "I think you have a perfect body. It's beautiful."

"Men's bodies aren't beautiful, you little idiot." He grinned. "But now this"—he let his gaze slowly traverse the length of her, staring pointedly at several parts of her anatomy along the way—"this is beautiful. I especially like these." He kissed each breast, then foraged a warm, moist trail over her midriff, across her stomach to her navel.

The pointed tip and its attention to that part of her had Shay wondering if something mysterious had occurred to her body. If the man so much as blinked at her, she thought wildly, she trembled or she groaned.

"Please!" she exclaimed through the misty veil of desire sucking her deeper and deeper into its inflexible grip.

"I love hearing you say that," Kurt rasped. "It makes me know I'm pleasing you. But we don't want to rush what's going to happen, honey, do we?" His deep voice caressed her. "Each moment, each second, has to be perfect." His mouth dipped farther then, his tongue finding that most sensitive place, and again exposed her to a such a blaze of passion and need, she began hearing soft whimpers that grew into louder cries of ecstasy. Somewhere in the maelstrom of emotion, she finally was able to discern that the sounds were coming from her.

Shay knew her hips were arching toward him . . . she was even aware of her hands clasping his head and pressing him against her —but she was helpless to control the jerky movements of her body. These were acts she'd never contemplated in her life, but nevertheless her reactions were as instinctive as if she'd practiced years and years for this moment. Her body was on a plane of unbelievable responsiveness to Kurt's will. He hinted, he suggested, he nudged, and her senses obeyed, her body eagerly complied. It was that simple. Simple, Shay thought, and incredibly beautiful.

When she thought she would pass out from the sheer wonderment of it all, she felt the warmth of his large body encompassing hers as he positioned himself over her. The thick, dark hair on his chest had always struck Shay as sexy, but to feel its bristly ends in contact with her nipples was unreal, and added a new dimension to excitement. The affect was mind boggling, she thought feverishly. In fact, she thought, smiling as she stared into Kurt's eyes, everything about this evening had taken on the veil of unreality.

"Please," she whispered, "if this is a dream, then don't let me wake up."

"It's no dream, kitten," Kurt said softly.

"Funny," she murmured lazily. "Tonight is the first time in years that you've called me kitten. It was your pet name for me when I was a little girl. But I've never felt more like a woman than I do at this moment. There's only one other thing left to make it complete."

"The faith you have in me makes me nervous as hell, honey," Kurt cautioned, seeing and reading the light in her eyes. Damn! She was still so innocent. At this moment she was as open and without deceit as a fresh spring shower . . . and she wanted him, and she had let him know. Kurt was touched. It had been a long time since he'd come face to face with such openness.

As for himself, Kurt found himself reverting back to the norm by emotionally erecting a protective wall around his feelings. Shay had gotten closer to him than anyone else, and he knew his relationship with her was unique. But he was leery of allowing even her to penetrate the barrier between his heart and the rest of the world. One part of him demanded that he protect Shay—the other part that he protect himself from her and the world at large.

Shay stretched like a sleek little cat, deliberately pressing her breasts closer to the hairy wall of his chest. "Please make love to me, Kurt."

He grinned down at her, cherishing the trust and adoration he saw shining in her lovely eyes. "Oh, I will, sweetheart, I most definitely will."

Kurt eased first one tanned, muscled leg and then the other between her slim thighs, the hardness of him seeking its hot, moist counterpart. He entered gently, then gave a quick, firm thrust to help minimize that brief moment of pain.

Shay grabbed at Kurt for a brief second and then was surprised when mild discomfort immediately flowed into the incredibly beautiful merging of their bodies. Even more passion snaked its way into her being, casting her up to the wonderful extreme reaches of passion. The only solid force within the madly spinning world was Kurt. She clung wildly to the strong hardness of him, the deep, rough caress of his voice always close to her ear.

When the sound of their voices crying out simultaneously registered with Shay, it brought a rush of tears to her eyes. For in that moment of climactic splendor she'd held him as he'd been holding her. They'd each given and had equally received. That realization would remain with her forever.

She drifted off to sleep with her hand clasped protectively to Kurt's perspiration-damp hair, a gentle smile on her lips.

Sometime during the night Shay was awakened by large hands caressing her breasts, then sweeping downward over the flatness of her stomach and below to cup the center of her desire. Warm lips captured first one nipple and then the other, till both tips were rigid with desire.

"Mmmmmm." She stretched luxuriously, rubbing the tumid peaks against Kurt's chest. "That feels delicious." She peered sleepily at him in the darkness. "Is this the norm?" she asked mischievously. "Do we make love, take a nap, and then make love again all night?"

Kurt laughed. "Believe it or not, there isn't a list of rules and guidelines a couple must abide by."

"Good. Because I much prefer what we do and what you do to me."

"Hmmm," he teased between playful nibbles at her bottom lip, "you're a picky little thing, aren't you?"

"Not really, just deliriously happy."

Kurt refrained from commenting. He wasn't ready to go into the reasons why their lives after tonight wouldn't necessarily be any different. He would still have his reservations, and she would have to face the reality of living out a childhood fantasy. Rather, he began coaxing her to the same excruciating level of ecstasy as before, then claimed her body and carried her away with him on a magic carpet of desire and passion that rocked the universe.

* * *

"What do you mean, you have to go out of town?" Shay asked as she sat in the middle of the bed with the sheet tucked under her arms. "You didn't mention anything about a trip last night."

There was a disquieting look about her sleep-kissed face that had Kurt clenching his fists to keep from crawling back into bed with her and staying there, making love for days.

"Conversation wasn't our strong suit last night," he said instead, forcing his voice to remain controlled. He finished tucking in the tail of his shirt, then sat on the edge of the bed and reached for his shoes and socks. "Do you have some particular reason why I shouldn't go out of town?"

"Certainly not," she muttered stonily. "Though I did think we might be able to have dinner together sometime during the next few days."

"Perhaps we can when I get back." He forced himself to look at her, telling himself not to let his resolve be swayed by the hurt look in her eyes. "I do remember telling you last night, honey, that life would go on after we made love. Well"—he gestured by slightly lifting one broad shoulder—"this is *afterward*— the harsh reality of daylight. If you look out the windows you'll find nothing significantly different this morning from any other morning."

145

"Then exactly what would you call what happened between us last night?" Shay demanded stubbornly.

Suddenly Kurt swung around, the unexpectedness of his move causing Shay to drop back against the mattress. He leaned over her, one large hand resting on either side of her head. "Last night was most probably something that shouldn't have happened at all," he rasped in a hard voice. "But it was something we both knew *was going* to happen from the day I hauled you out of that damned bathtub, didn't we?" At her big-eyed, barely audible, "Yes," Kurt went on.

"It's not that I'm trying to run away from this . . . chemistry between us, Shay, but I refuse to be railroaded into a situation I'm leery of."

"Railroaded!" burst from Shay's lips, that being the only word that had clearly registered with her. "Just what do you mean by railroaded?"

Kurt frowned at her. "I mean that you want to think of last night as the beginning of a future for us, Shay. That's fine . . . for you, but not me."

Shay shook her head. "You know last night was fantastic . . . and everything that happened between us was fantastic. But you're so afraid of committing even a small part of yourself to a woman, that you'll deny us both a

146

chance at happiness." She paused, glaring at him. "You're a flaming coward, Kurt Barron!"

"Oh?" he remarked mockingly. "Is that what you think? Are you so naive as to think that one night of lovemaking will automatically wipe away all problems between two people?"

"Certainly not, but—"

"There are no buts about it, honey. Sex should not be used between two people as a shoring-up device like some sort of adhesive."

Shay stared disgustedly at him. "What the hell are you rambling on about? And will you please tell me exactly what it is that we're suppose to be attempting to 'shore up'?"

Kurt pushed himself away from her, his features settling in an immovable mask. He threw her an irritated glare as he grabbed up his jacket and slung it over one shoulder. "I can see now there's no reasoning with you. You're determined to regard life and everything in it through those damned rose-colored glasses that are permanently attached to your eyes!"

Shay bounded to her feet, keeping herself covered by the sheet and whipping the ends in order like a tiny tornado. How dare he stand there and accuse her of such damned nonsense? "I may view the world differently than you, Mr. Barron," she said icily, "but it's a damned sight better than thinking every person who gets within a mile of me is going to try to shaft me." She stalked toward the bathroom.

"Please close the door on your way out," she threw at him just before she slammed the door shut.

As she adjusted the shower, then dropped the sheet and stepped beneath the water, Shay was barely able to contain her anger. How dare he! she thought furiously . . . how dare he! He'd made it sound as if he'd done her a tremendous favor by making love to her for an entire night. As if he'd participated solely because she was "little Shay" and he was supposed to "look after" her. What a crock!

But during the time it took her to complete her shower, dress, and straighten up the room, Shay found most of her anger toward Kurt evaporating. She also remembered what Jane had said during one of their talks, about what a complex person she considered Kurt to be. Shay was beginning to see the wisdom of her sister's opinion. Kurt was complex . . . as well as stubborn as a mule. She sighed.

Yet no matter how she rationalized both sides of the issue, she still came up with some of the same conclusions in the end, the most important one being how much she cared for Kurt.

Suddenly Shay came to a stop in the middle of making the bed. She also remembered something else Jane had said on that same day weeks ago. She'd asked Shay if she was in love with Kurt.

"I can't be," Shay muttered, "I simply can't be." But the warm rush of feeling that swept over her at the thought of such a thing being so was too pointed to ignore. "Well, if I am," she murmured, chewing thoughtfully at the inside of her bottom lip, "I sure do feel sorry for me. Getting that thick-headed ass to admit to even a preference in food takes the finesse of an ambassador." A grin of satisfaction settled over her attractive features as a whole new world of thought and ideas and nights with Kurt became focused in her mind. "Imagine what it will be like when I tell him that I won't force a huge wedding on him, and that I'm open to all suggestions for a honeymoon."

Kurt stood in his bathroom and stared at his reflection with total and complete disgust.

"What the flaming hell happened to me last night?" he asked incredulously. "Did my brain go on vacation and leave my libido in charge? Damn!" He closed his eyes as he thought of what had occurred and how soft and right Shay had felt in his arms.

But the other half of Kurt's brain knew that soft and warm can also mean a well-hidden bomb. I really take the cake for making stupid mistakes where Shay is concerned. I screwed up a beautiful relationship by not being able to keep my hands off her. If there was an idiot of the year award, Kurt continued flogging himself, I would win hands down.

But there was yet another more shocking realization coursing its way into Kurt's thoughts. He shook his head in disbelief. In his . . . er . . . haste to get to Shay the evening before, the thought of any kind of protection had been the farthest thing from his mind. He was also fairly certain she wasn't on the pill. That being the case—he sighed roughly—he might have settled both their futures once and for all.

CHAPTER EIGHT

Shay lifted the receiver to her ear with two fingers, muttering all the while about people with the incredibly bad timing to call when she was up to her elbows in mixing potting soil.

"Hello?" she said crisply.

"My, my." Jane chuckled. "Don't you sound brisk. Having a bad day?"

"Whatever makes you think that?" Shay grinned. "Hold on a sec." She let the receiver slide down the front of her protective smock while she slipped her hands out of the thick cloth gloves she was wearing. She cradled the receiver between her cheek and shoulder. "Now. What can I do for you?"

"Have lunch with me today?"

"Ohhh, Jane." Shay sighed. "I'm practically swimming in potting soil. Let me take a rain check please?"

"No," Jane said stubbornly. "For the last few days you've been living like a hermit. I know

Becky is away on one of her jaunts, so that means you haven't seen anybody."

"I see people." Shay laughed. "When I'm making the rounds checking on my plants, I see lots of people."

"Strangers. They don't count. You need to be around your loved ones."

"Why?"

"Don't be deliberately obtuse, Shay," she was told in a crisp tone. "You haven't been yourself lately. Ted and I decided that we should keep a closer check on you," she added slyly.

"Are you afraid I'm going nuts? That I'll undress in public or something equally 'terrible'?"

"Oh, don't be such a pain in the behind. You know we love you. And so does your niece, who you haven't seen in weeks. Don't you feel ashamed of yourself for neglecting her?"

"I do not neglect Susie. Besides, she's enough like me to know I love her. She doesn't need me standing over her twenty-four hours a day telling her so."

"Mmmm . . . I'm afraid you're right. She does bear a strong resemblance to you in temperament. Stubborn as the devil. What time shall I pick you up?"

"When?"

"Today, silly, for lunch."

"Twelve-thirty," Shay replied through gritted teeth, knowing full well her sister detested eating lunch a second past twelve noon.

"Fine," Jane said frostily, then plunked down the receiver.

"Damnation!" Shay yelled as she practically threw the receiver into its cradle. "I think I'll move to Australia. There are times when I literally detest family." She glanced at her watch and grimaced. Only an hour and a half left before darling Jane would arrive.

She pulled her gloves back on, and began attacking the soil she was mixing as if it were personally responsible for all her problems. Sisters and sexy, stubborn neighbors, she began in a silent litany. Those two things were probably at the root of every problem to befall man.

Jane popped the bite of cottage cheese into her mouth and continued to regard Shay with open speculation.

"Is there potting soil on my face?" Shay asked, holding her napkin in readiness to perform a quick cleanup.

"No."

"Oh." She frowned as she continued to eat her steak and baked potato. After another few minutes of enduring this close and thoroughly annoying examination, she laid down her fork and gave her sister a murderous glare. "Will you please tell me why you're subjecting me to that gimlet-eyed stare?"

"Was I staring?" Jane asked innocently. "Sorry, my mind was on something else."

"What?" Shay countered, not in the least believing her.

"Kurt."

"What about him?"

"I was just thinking how remarkable it is that both of you seem afflicted with the same condition."

"What condition?" Shay asked suspiciously.

"Edginess. The night of Margetta's party he was like a cat on a hot woodstove. Plus, he couldn't keep his eyes off you. If I'd been his date, I would have murdered him. Come to think of it"—Jane smiled smugly—"he left her at the party shortly after Ted took you home."

"So?"

"So"—Jane gestured—"nothing. It just struck me as odd that you and Kurt left round about the same time. Did he come over to your place when he got home?"

Shay sat back in her chair, her face screwed up into her usual pose of bottom lip caught between her teeth and her brow furrowed when she was contemplating something important or something as casual as strangling her sister. "You are, without a doubt, the nosiest human being—besides Kurt Barron—it has ever been my misfortune to meet. Don't you ever get ashamed of yourself for prying into my private life?"

"Don't be ridiculous," Jane huffed in an affronted tone of voice. "Being nosy has nothing to do with anything. We're sisters, and I'm the oldest. That gives me the right to watch after you. You aren't exactly known for your levelheadedness, you know. I worry because you only eat if someone happens to remind you. You'd stay in that darned greenhouse forever if Kurt or I didn't pull you out."

"Poor Jane. What a cross you must bear." Shay chuckled. "Now that you've pointed out a number of my shortcomings, I know why I avoid having lunch with you, sister dear. Added to your unflattering habit of wanting to know all about my business, you are always casting aspersions on my mental capabilities. If I weren't positive it was all being done in the name of love, I'd never speak to you again. Now," Shay said in a very seriously comical manner, "tell me again what it is you want to know."

"You're a nut." Jane grinned. She was silent for a moment, then asked, "Did Kurt come over to see you after the party?"

"Yes, he did."

"Oh, good. That means I win."

"Win what?"

"Ted and I had a bet going. He said the two of you were fighting and Kurt wouldn't dare show his face at your door that evening. I said that the two of you had been fighting for as long as I could remember, and I bet him twenty dollars Kurt made a beeline for your house as soon as he left here. Was I correct?"

"Yes."

"Fantastic! How long did he stay?"

"All night."

"Great. Just wait till I tell Te— Did you say all night, Shay?" Jane asked in a hushed voice, her eyes round as saucers.

"Yes." Shay nodded, the expression on her face not giving anything away, then sat forward in her chair, her forearms resting on the edge of the table. "Let me ask you something. How would you like to have Kurt as your brother-in-law?"

"Oh, dear Lord!" Jane moaned. She, too, leaned forward, one hand nervously fingering the pearls at her neck. "You didn't . . . I mean you aren't . . . I mean . . . Oh, Shay." She exhaled long and nervously. "I can't think straight."

"Well, my goodness, Clara Jane, I thought I was the only one of us whose mental faculties were impaired."

"Oh, don't be such a nerd," Jane said sharply, "and for heaven's sake don't call me by that ridiculous name. Could you have gotten pregnant?" she asked, changing the subject without the slightest warning. "Don't worry." She patted Shay's hand consolingly. "I'll go to him and demand he do the right thing by you."

"Really?" Shay nodded, thinking this was beginning to turn into a really neat lunch. She'd set out only to irritate Jane because she'd been forced into accepting the invitation, but now it was definitely beginning to show possibilities. She could just see Kurt facing an angry Jane, demanding matrimony on every front. "He's not home at the moment, but I'll be sure to let you know as soon as he returns."

"Do that," she was briskly instructed.

"But I feel I must tell you, Jane. I'm not pregnant . . . at least I don't think so. And you really shouldn't get involved, you know."

Jane looked stricken, her pretty face framed by her dark hair, a study of concern. "Oh, honey. How can you be so blasé about something so serious? Don't answer." She patted Shay's hand again. "You don't have to say another word. And, yes, I will get involved. . . . I must, because I know exactly what happened. Kurt took advantage of you, didn't he?"

"Not exactly," Shay said simply. "I didn't put up the slightest hint of a fight, Janey. It was something we both enjoyed."

"Nevertheless," Jane remarked determinedly, her dark eyes agleam with dedicated purpose. She was on a crusade to right a wrong that had been done her sister. "I'll make him see his responsibilities. You just leave everything to me."

"Of course." Shay leaned back and nodded,

gesturing with her hands. "Why didn't I think of that? You're the oldest . . . you just told me that."

Later, after she had finally gotten away from Jane, and was back in her greenhouse working, Shay got a surprise phone call from Kurt.

"Yes?" she spoke in a tight, cold voice once she learned the identity of the caller. Jane's zany reaction had, for a moment, made the serious situation rather comical because of her sincere belief that Shay had been *wronged*. But talking directly to the culprit was far from humorous, Shay concluded.

"How are you?" Kurt asked, wincing at the coldness of her voice. He'd been worrying about her nonstop since he'd left Flagstaff. He'd picked up the phone numerous times to call her, but hadn't worked up the nerve till now. And wasn't that a hell of a note, he thought derisively. He stood over six feet three inches, was worth more than he could ever spend, pursued by countless women, and was being intimidated by a five-feet-one-inch, blue-eyed minx.

"What's that suppose to mean?" Shay deliberately baited him.

"You know damn well what it means!" Kurt stormed. "Are you feeling okay? The person inquiring expects an answer that will let him know whether or not the person he's inquiring about is ill, in trouble, or feeling bad in general. Now," he fairly roared, "how the hell are you?"

"None of your damned business!" Shay roared right back. She banged down the receiver, then crossed her arms over her waist and glared at it.

Within less than a minute the phone was ringing again. She answered in her softest, nicest business voice. "Shay's Flowers."

"If you hang up on me again, I'll fly home and burn down that damned greenhouse. Understand?"

"Certainly," she replied indifferently. "Just because I despise you doesn't mean I'm deaf."

"You do not despise me, nor I you. I don't know what the hell we do feel yet, but I'm working on it."

"I can hardly wait for your earth-shattering discovery. In the meantime, would you please state your business, Mr. Barron? I'm trying to finish replanting that huge, empty planter in your office."

"When do you think you'll be through?" he posed the question swiftly. If it hadn't been for the damn merger he'd been working on for months, he'd be in his office right now. He might even have been able to make her see his point of view regarding their relationship . . . if it could be called such. He really couldn't be sure. At the moment it resembled a battlefield.

"Another couple of days. Why?"

"No reason."

Shay was dying to ask him when he'd be home, but pride wouldn't let her. In the past few weeks she'd had more rebuffs from Kurt Barron than she'd encountered in her entire life. In the three days he'd been away, she'd finally convinced herself to let him do the chasing from now on. Which meant, she'd also told herself, that whatever might have been between them, was now well and truly lost. Kurt had been cold and distant the morning after their lovemaking. He seemed unable and unwilling to share in a warm, loving relationship.

"What have you been doing this week?" he ventured, breaking the tense silence.

"Nothing much," she said without thinking, then could have socked herself for being so open. She should have told him she'd been out till all hours every night he'd been away, she thought furiously. "I met Jane for lunch today. She . . . er . . . asked about you."

"I'll remember to give her a call when I get back. She's one of my favorite people."

She'd love to be a fly on the wall and hear the conversation. Shay all but laughed. "I really do need to get back to work, Kurt."

"Goodby, kitten. Take care of yourself."

"Bye." Again Shay replaced the receiver, but this time a little more gently. It was difficult to remain angry at someone she cared for, she thought heavily as she returned to work.

160

Especially when it's someone you love, that annoying little voice of hers whispered.

I do not love Kurt Barron, Shay argued, mixing the soil with renewed strength. I do not love him. The very thought of her doing such a silly, useless thing caused her knees to go weak. That would be terrible . . . disastrous.

It suddenly occurred to Shay that she was shivering. She paused in her work to touch the back of her wrist to her cheek. Skin against skin was like two cubes of ice touching. She removed the gloves, then stepped back and began briskly rubbing her arms.

What she was feeling was eerie and unreal . . . there was no sane explanation for it. All she was *really* aware of was a certain presence around her, a presence that made her know Kurt might be hundreds of miles away in Washington, but part of him was in the room with her.

"Heavens," she murmured shakily, looking around her as if expecting him to materialize any second. "Maybe Jane is right. Maybe I am crazy." She turned and headed for the door. "I need a break."

That evening, after a leisurely bath and a light supper, Shay decided it was about time she went through her cupboard and made a grocery list. Since it had been over a month since her last extensive shopping spree, she was honestly surprised to find anything edible in the house.

As she slowly made her way down aisle after aisle of the supermarket, she couldn't help but shudder when she considered what her purchases were going to do to her bank balance. She wondered why she didn't just give up eating all together. It was an expensive habit.

Shay loaded her groceries into the van, then, as she began the trip back home, she found herself wanting the season to hurry along. She was ready for some skiing. The slopes were an excellent place to forget problems. One problem with that brilliant thought was, Kurt had been with her on no telling how many skiing jaunts. Even that pleasurable solitude of sorts was denied her.

As Shay rounded the corner of her street, situated near the outskirts of town, she immediately saw yellow flashing lights atop long vehicles she recognized as fire trucks.

"What the . . ." she began, slowly driving a little closer, only to realize that the commotion was at her house. "My God!"

She slammed on the brakes, opened the door, and bounded from the van like a tiny whirlwind. Thick whitish, grayish hoses were strewn every which way, causing Shay to stumble as she hurried along. As she neared the house, she recognized several of her neighbors standing helplessly by.

Mrs. Abbot, her neighbor two doors down, turned and saw Shay. The older woman rushed to her side and put her arms around her. "Oh, my dear, I'm so sorry. They're hoping to contain it to the kitchen. You might want to talk with them, but be careful, dear."

"Thank you, Mrs. Abbot." She nodded grimly as she hurried along, the sympathetic faces of other neighbors and their kind words falling on deaf ears. Shay wanted to get to her greenhouse. It was imperative that she do so. There were things in the house that she cared about, she thought numbly, but it was her flowers and plants that she was most concerned about.

"Just a minute, miss," a fireman called out. "I'm afraid we can't allow you to go any farther."

"But you don't understand," Shay cried, glancing at the face smeared with soot and sweat, then to the greenhouse a good way behind the house. "I must get back there. That's my livelihood."

"We've already checked the greenhouse, miss, and everything seems to be okay. You'd help out a lot more if you'd just wait out front with the others. We still have a long way to go to get this taken care of."

"Can you tell where it began?"

"From the looks of it, miss, I'd say it started in the kitchen. I think we'll be able to contain it to that area." He turned as someone came rushing up to him. "Sorry, miss. I've got to go."

Shay watched him hurry away with sinking dismay, then focused again on the smoldering mess that only a mere hour and a half ago had been her home.

CHAPTER NINE

Every second of his return flight found Kurt with very little else on his mind but Shay.

Shay.

God! She was driving him out of his mind. Never in his entire life had he in any way resembled an oaf . . . until lately.

Every time he tried to talk with her, no matter how fervently he promised himself to keep calm, his temper would erupt like the outpourings of a boiling volcano. Shay would react in kind, and they would wind up nose to nose in a hard-hitting game of insults.

He shook his head. Dammit. That had to stop. Constantly fighting with someone you loved . . .

Kurt tucked his stubborn chin, his lips drawn in a straight line, his brows bunched together over his dark eyes. Retrospection, he decided irritably—especially in one's own case—was one hell of a bitter dose. Why did it always have to make one look like a total fool?

By the time he was one block from his home, Kurt had firmly decided that he *definitely* didn't love Shay Michaels. At least not in the sense of a lover. But she *was* his lover . . . or she had been, he argued. Nonsense, the firmer, more reasonable side of him riposted. The two of you spent the night together . . . you *made* love together. It was great. Now let it be.

Good advice. Kurt nodded thoughtfully. Good advice indeed. He wouldn't even bother to call Shay when he got to his house. He would wait and see how she wanted to handle the next move. After all, he was quietly congratulating himself, he was older, more mature. He was nearly fourteen years older than Shay, and certainly wiser when it came to affairs. His experience and ability to control situations would see them through the rough spots of the next few weeks. Of that he was confident.

Kurt rounded the corner to his street, his sense of expectation zooming upward like the mercury on a thermometer that has been plunged into a pan of boiling water. But as he drew abreast of the small house that was his neighbor on the left, his heart lurched into his throat at the same moment his long narrow foot, shod in Gucci loafers, hit the brakes!

He asked the obvious question ("What the hell?") out loud, his stunned gaze staring disbelievingly at the disreputable condition of Shay's house.

The section of roof over the kitchen and laundry room was a charred mess. There was a wide square of heavy-duty plastic covering a huge hole over the dining room, and it looked as if most of the windows in the back part of the house—at least the ones he could see from the street—were broken. Pieces of plywood had been nailed over the openings.

Shay!

All sorts of pictures of her lying in some hospital with burns over her beautiful young body sent Kurt's blood pressure rocketing. It couldn't be. It simply couldn't be, he told himself. "No!" he murmured in an agonized voice.

He jammed his foot to the floor and sent the car hurtling into his driveway like a runaway train. He was out and running toward the front door without even turning off the engine.

By the time he had Jane on the line, Kurt's hands were clammy with nervous perspiration —in fact, his entire body was clammy. It was as if someone had totally immersed him in a tub of water.

"Where the hell is Shay?" he yelled the moment Jane said hello.

"Kurt?" Then she almost laughed out loud at the question in her voice. She'd know his voice anywhere in the world. "I suppose you saw the house?" she said quietly.

"Never mind the damned house, Jane. Tell me about Shay," he snapped, the panic he was experiencing lending a glacial iciness to his voice. "Was she injured?"

"No, no," Jane quickly assured him. "In fact, she was at the grocery store when the fire started. She's taken a one-bedroom apartment in that new, expensive complex. The one with all the open beams and fireplaces. I know that place has to be expensive. I just don't understand why Shay wouldn't move in with us. Do you know the place?"

"I should," Kurt answered in a far less intense voice than a moment ago, "I own them. I also agree with you about the apartment. There's five bedrooms and four baths in this damn house. Why didn't she just move in here? She has a key."

"You'll have to ask her that," Jane said soothingly, privately thinking that if she were in Shay's shoes, she'd sooner move in with a raging bull elephant than Kurt Barron. "Changing her mind is like tearing down the Great Wall of China."

"Don't I know it," Kurt agreed, relieved yet defeated.

"Er . . . Kurt," Jane said hesitantly. "May I ask you a very . . . very personal question?"

"Sure, kid, shoot."

"Shay and I had lunch together a couple of days ago, and I'm worried about her. We also had a long . . . long talk. Some of the things she revealed shocked me, I suppose . . . and then again, maybe they didn't. I'm doing a really poor job of this." She paused, looking upward beseechingly. Please, she silently prayed, if I've ever needed help, I need it now. "What I'm trying to say is—is the relationship between you and Shay serious? Rather, is it serious to you?"

"Damn, Janey." Kurt chuckled. "Are you asking what my intentions toward your sister are?"

"Yes." She sighed, thinking she might just as well jump in with both feet. She hated to reveal that Shay had, so to speak, spilled the beans, but her sister's happiness was involved —and, if she were honest, so was Kurt's. But Jane couldn't help but feel Kurt was in a far better position to look after himself than Shay. "I suppose I am. I must admit I wasn't totally surprised by certain . . . er . . . aspects of your relationship that Shay revealed. She's always adored you. But still and all, I worry about her."

Kurt was secretly relieved by Jane's questioning. At least now he could talk to somebody about Shay. "When I first became aware of how she *thinks* she feels about me, and knowing her propensity for changing her mind and the men in her life, I asked her to wait six months. If, after that length of time passed, she still felt the same way, then we would go from there. But with our tempers and certain other little incidents that came up between us, the six-month probation period was shot to hell before it ever got off the ground. We can't discuss what's happened between us or how either of us feels without it turning into a battle. Frankly . . . for once in my life, I'm at a loss as to what to do."

"Well, don't worry," Jane ruefully remarked. "I'm sure Shay will think of something. There's just one other thing on my mind, Kurt."

"Let's have it," he told her.

"I don't want to see Shay hurt. I know she's impetuous, and at times she can drive you up the wall. On the other hand, you *are* much older and more experienced."

"In other words," Kurt inserted dryly, "you're holding me responsible. Right?"

"Not entirely," Jane said honestly. "But neither do I think you're completely innocent."

Kurt assured her he understood, and that if he were in her position he would probably feel the same way. After a few more moments of conversation they hung up and he hurried back to his car.

Kurt was anxious to go over to Shay's apartment and see for himself that she was okay. Shay wasn't just another woman to him. She'd been a virgin when they made love, and even though they argued and fought like hell, she trusted him. Jane's case also was different. She wasn't just some nosy piker taking great delight in prying into his personal life. She and Shay were close . . . for sisters their relationship was rather unique, they were best friends as well.

See, his voice of caution warned, nothing about this affair is as it should be. This is the first time you've ever been called on the carpet, so to speak, over sleeping with a woman.

But we didn't just sleep together, Kurt quickly refuted, and it isn't just an affair. That was not what he was having with Shay, he insisted stubbornly as he cut in and out of traffic, oblivious to the horn blasts of other drivers. It went far beyond a mere affair, dammit. When there was love between two people, the relationship became more meaningful . . . very special.

Phillip Norcross sat back in the oxblood-colored leather chair, his lips thoughtfully pursed as he held the receiver between his cheek and shoulder, and listened.

"I'm tired of this cat-and-mouse game we're playing," the caller warned Phillip. "You've changed your mind three times since our original deal. I'm ready to spend some of Nicholas Pappolas's money."

"You'd better be glad I have changed my mind," Phillip said scathingly. "If we'd tried to pass you off as my long-lost cousin, as you were

171

so intent upon doing at first, we would be facing all kinds of problems at the moment."

"What's that crack supposed to mean?"

"The detective Uncle Nicholas hired is smarter than I thought. Apparently he's uncovered the same information my man unearthed. Consequently, my uncle has been apprised of said information, and has been told that, barring death or some other misfortune, he will in all probability be united with his illegitimate offspring in the very near future," he explained sourly.

"How touching," his friend muttered. "In the meantime, where does that leave me? I hope you aren't so stupid as to think what little bit of money you've given me is enough to keep my mouth shut forever. After all, before you lost your nerve, we had much larger plans."

"That's a damned lie!" Phillip snarled. "I did not lose my nerve."

"Call it what you will. But you are the one who continued holding back, who said it wasn't the right time to make the hit on your uncle. Now he's taken matters into his own hands and we're left holding the bag . . . rather, you are. I still expect to get a sizable compensation for the time and trouble I've been put to. I'll be talking to you in a few days, Phillip," he was told, and then the line went dead.

Phillip stared at the receiver, then cradled it,

the expression on his face and in his eyes . . . murderous.

He got to his feet and walked over to the window and stared out. He'd known for months that his uncle had an heir. Since that time, somewhere in the back of his mind, he'd also thought it would be fairly easy, by whatever means, to keep that relationship from ever becoming known by either party. Keeping Nicholas ignorant of his child, Phillip reasoned, kept his own position in the company secure, and also assured Phillip a greater share in the company upon Nicholas's death.

As he stared broodingly at the New York skyline, he knew there were only two people standing between him and what *should*—what *would*—be his rightful inheritance. His so-called partner and the illegitimate cousin he had yet to meet. And, Phillip decided, since he wasn't overly fond of either, he was terribly afraid accidents of a very serious nature would have to be arranged for them.

Yes indeed. He smiled thinly as he turned from the window, rubbing his hands together in an anticipatory gesture. Accidents ingeniously planned . . . and perfectly executed.

Kurt pressed one square-tipped finger against the black button, then just as quickly raised his fist and rapped it against the door.

173

"All right! All right!" He grinned when he heard the irritated sound of Shay's voice.

When the door was flung open, Kurt just stood staring at her, a hand braced on either side of the aperture. His deep, dark eyes pored over every inch of her, from her bare toes peeking out from beneath the edges of her robe, the red one Kurt recognized, to the shining cap of curly brown hair. There was such a vulnerable look about her, such an open expression of wanting him in her face, that Kurt felt his huge body go weak.

"At least your favorite robe wasn't scorched," he teased, remembering the last times he'd seen her in it.

She tipped her head to one side and pretended to be insulted. "Only Agatha's diamonds outclass this lovely creation."

"I . . . I was scared as hell when I saw your house." The gruffness of his voice washed over her and healed the wounds brought about by fear and frustration and loneliness.

Shay softly smiled. "I called your office and left word with that new and irritating secretary you've hired that I was fine. I even gave her this address. Just in case you decided to come calling," she added pertly. "Although I honestly wasn't expecting you for at least two days."

"I didn't plan on being back for at least two more days."

"Then why are you?"

"I missed you."

"That's a good start, Kurtland," she teased. "But you still have a long way to go."

Kurt stepped inside and closed the door behind him, then slowly gathered her in his arms till every inch of her body was in direct contact with his, and his long, shuddered sigh was the only sound in the room for a moment or two. "Is your roommate home?"

"No. I don't expect her back till tomorrow."

"Good. I'll think about how far I have to go, after we make love."

"Just a minute, Mr. Barron." Shay tried for a serious mien. "Do you honestly expect me to allow you to knock on my door, tell me you missed me, then take me to bed? All within a space of five minutes?"

"Precisely."

"Oh," she murmured with a grin, then tried to keep a straight face as she pretended to be deeply studying the proposition. "Mr. Barron, honey, I do like your style." She chuckled as she was swept up into his arms and carried from the room.

CHAPTER TEN

When Kurt set her on her feet beside the bed in the dimly lit room, they each began undressing. There were no words passed between them; none were needed. It was as if everything they felt for each other, each emotion, each infinitesimal thought or sigh, was reflected in their faces as their eyes met, as their gazes swept over each other's body.

When the last bit of clothing was added to the carelessly strewn garments on the floor, Kurt reached out and clasped his palms to Shay's waist, his gaze intent as he studied her face.

He drew a ragged breath at what he saw there. "We're both gluttons for punishment, aren't we?"

Shay reached up and placed two of her fingers against his lips. "Shhh." She smiled. "Don't start taking the moment apart. Just enjoy it."

Her fingers left his face to skim rather hesitantly across his skin, touching the hair-roughened surface of his chest, the tautness of his midriff and abdomen, following the narrowing V of dark hair to where it disappeared and the hardness of his manhood beckoned the whisper of her touch.

Kurt, who had been standing like a statue beneath the less than practiced, but lethal, ministrations of her caresses, uttered a low groan of intense pleasure mingled with the pain of desire. His large hands clutched the swell of her buttocks and pulled her against him, his mouth seeking and finding her open one.

Their tongues met, retreated, then became engaged in the same potent duel as their bodies—tempting, teasing, and then beginning the erotic process all over again. He bent down, clasped his arms around Shay, then raised her so that her breasts were on level with his mouth. Immediately one pink nipple disappeared between his lips.

Shay felt each pull of his lips in concert with a corresponding sensation in the lower part of her abdomen. Her head tipped forward, her forehead resting against his hair. Then her breath caught in her throat as she felt herself slipping downward; the sensations of skin and hair rubbing and caressing and of the slight abrasiveness had her grasping at Kurt for support when her feet were back on solid ground.

But instead of taking her then, he went to his knees, his mouth and tongue seeking that part of her waiting to sheath him in its wealth of mysterious fire and exquisite softness.

When Shay thought she couldn't stand another second of the indescribable torment, Kurt rose to his feet. They fell to the bed, the prolonged punishment of deliberately holding back adding a feverish urgency to their gestures, their hands. They were hungry for each other and it was manifested in their movements.

Kurt parted her thighs and settled over her, his hands cupping her face. "I can't even begin to understand this hold you have on me." His eyes were dark, watchful pools boring into Shay's very soul.

She caught and held her breath as he began slowly to enter her. As he lowered his head and traced his tongue across her lips, she gasped, and let herself flow with the shimmers of seemingly endless beauty and contentment hitting her one after the other.

They went as one into a world where emotions become stark and bare and where touch is so intense as to be almost painful in its ecstacy, forgetting the battle of pride and fear and misunderstanding that stood between them.

Later, having emerged weak but sated, they

slept. When they awoke they talked, beginning with the subject of the house.

"Did they give you any idea what started it?" Kurt asked. He was half sitting, his head and shoulders resting against the headboard, with Shay's head on his shoulder. "Did you leave some electrical appliance on or something on the stove?"

"Nothing that I can remember. Apparently they think it was the wiring," she replied during a huge yawn. "I'm just glad it happened when it did, and not in the middle of the night. I might not have woken up."

"Don't say things like that." Kurt groaned, his arm lying across her shoulder tightening painfully.

Shay chuckled as she raised her head and peeked at his stern expression. She reached up and tweaked his considerable nose. "Don't take everything so seriously, Kurtland," she teased him in her best "Agatha" voice. "We could spend hours going over what 'could have happened.'"

Kurt pressed her head against his chest and rested his chin on her hair. "I may be morbid as hell, honey, but when I rounded that corner and saw your house gutted, I damn near passed out. I'm afraid I'll be thinking about what 'could have happened' for quite a while."

"You know something, Kurt Barron?"

"Mmmm." He yawned, stretching his well-muscled arms over his head. "I'm not sure I want to hear this. You sound ominous."

"And you sound like a coward," Shay countered sternly. "But that wasn't what I had in mind."

"Really?" Kurt spoke softly against her ear, just before he pulled her around so that she was lying on top of him. "Now." He grinned. "Let me hear the worst."

. "I know why the fire threw you into such a panic."

"Why?"

"Because you love me."

"Well, of course I love you, you silly little goose." He frowned. What the hell was she getting at this time? The fingers of one wide hand idly flipped the ends of an errant lock of hair that had fallen against her cheek.

She caught his stubborn chin and forced him to look her straight in the eye. "There is love, Kurt, and there is love. You used to love me with the same kind of love one has for their favorite puppy dog. Now that love has changed to something a bit more intense. . . . Do you get my drift?"

Kurt regarded her steadily, his enigmatic expression giving nothing away. "I've never seen anyone so single minded about something in my entire life." He scowled.

"Oh, really?" Shay asked sharply. She wiggled around till she was sitting in the middle of the bed, with a handful of the sheet clutched to her bosom. "Why did you rush over here like a shot?"

"How about . . . I was worried about you?"

"How would you like a swift kick in the behind?" she countered sweetly. "For once in your womanizing life, Kurt Barron, why not tell the simple truth?"

"I'm not accustomed to having a woman stand over me with a gun and demand that I tell her I love her."

"I'm not just any woman, Mr. Barron," she said haughtily, "and there'll be no need for the gun if you cooperate. Otherwise, you just might find a doctor picking bird-shot out of your buns."

Kurt grinned. He couldn't help it. Damned if she wasn't about as determined a little thing as he'd ever run into. Funny, he thought as he rubbed a hand over his chin and watched her, she seemed to have given new meaning to the word *stubborn.*

"Are you trying to tell me that I'm . . . er . . . off limits . . . to other women?" he hedged. For the moment he decided to humor her. Later he'd break the news to her that he didn't allow any woman—even her—free run of his life.

"Not at all," Shay practically floored him by blithely announcing. "No more than I'm going to sit home and wait for you to call. I simply

181

wanted you to know that someday, when I'm ready to settle down, I'll pack a bag, and collect you and a marriage license. We'll be married, go on a blast of a honeymoon, then settle here or wherever . . . and live happily ever after."

"How nice of you to let me know 'our' plans," he remarked sourly.

Shay smiled. "I think so." She glanced around her, then back to Kurt. "Are you staying the night?"

"Gee," he said sarcastically. "Do you mean I can leave whenever I choose?"

She reached over and patted his cheek that felt bristly to her palm from the need of a shave. "Tsk. Tsk. You shouldn't be so petty, sweetheart. It causes your facial features to tighten, thereby creating new little lines. And considering that you're already several years older than me, I don't think you want to hasten the aging process, do you?"

"Dammit!" Kurt exclaimed, bounding to his feet in one quick move. "That is about the most asinine thing I've ever heard you say, lady. Let me 'hasten' "—he mimicked her use of the word—"to inform you that I look upon the state of matrimony with about as much affection as I would being thrown buck naked into a briar patch."

"How painful." Shay shuddered, deliberately teasing him. She was in seventh heaven. Never in her entire life had she seen Kurt more

182

upset than he was at this very moment. And he deserves every ounce of misery he's suffering, she thought gleefully. He's a first class rat!

"Don't interrupt me," he ordered her. "And another thing, I will not be told who I can or cannot see." He leaned down and leered at her. "I—like—women. All of them."

"That's good, Kurt," Shay replied undaunted. "I think it's healthy from an emotional standpoint for a man to have experience. On the other hand," she went on, "in light of certain elements of danger lurking in our society, I would advise you to use extreme caution when you're pursuing your . . . women."

"You're sick!"

"Oh, no," Shay quickly defended her stand, even though she was about to choke with laughter. "I'm in love . . . with you."

She scooted back till she was against the headboard and watched the man who had just made love to her, dress in record time. When he stood, after putting on his socks and shoes and reached for his jacket, Shay said, "You put your shirt on wrong side out."

Kurt glared at her. "I like it that way," he said savagely. He turned on his heel and stomped from the room. Seconds later Shay smiled contentedly as she heard the slamming of the front door.

She congratulated herself on the way things were working out. It wouldn't be long at all before poor Kurt would be putty in her hands. Yes indeed—she sighed as she laced her fingers together across her midriff and relaxed—mere putty in her hands.

Ian Denton sat quietly as Nicholas Pappolas read the report Ian had handed him only moments before. It had been an interesting case, one the detective had really enjoyed. Of course, Ian silently mused, having solved the case as well gave an extra boost to his pride. It had taken some fancy maneuvering on his part to provide Nicholas finally with what he wanted. Ian hoped the end results would give the man the happiness he was seeking.

Nicholas finished the cover note, then looked up, his gaze meeting that of Ian's. "I feel as if I'm about to open Pandora's box, Mr. Deaton. God knows, I haven't meant to harm anyone by trying to find my child."

"You made your decision the day you hired me to work for you, Mr. Pappolas. But read the report," Ian urged him, "then make up your mind as to whether or not you want to go farther. You still have time to back off."

Nicholas's hands trembled as he began reading the neatly typed words that would tell him whether or not he had a child. It had been part of the agreement with Ian Deaton that that information would be revealed *only* in the final report. And now, Nicholas reasoned, he was about to learn the truth. Had Emily been carrying his child as he'd suspected that day years ago in San Francisco, or had it been nothing more than his imagination?

He read . . . greedily at first, then more slowly. As he did so, his throat became dry, and for a moment the words on the legal-sized page swam before his eyes. His breathing seemed restricted and the sound of his heartbeat was drumming in his ears. For a moment Nicholas was fearful of passing out.

He placed a trembling hand to his forehead, unable, momentarily, to cope with what was being revealed to him.

He had a child. He—Nicholas Pappolas—had fathered a child. He dropped back against the high back of the soft leather, his face ashen.

Ian Deaton had seen all kinds of reactions in the many years of his career, and the tall, distinguished gentleman seated across the desk from him was one of the few clients the detective had come to like. At the moment he was more than a little worried.

"Can I get you a glass of water, Mr. Pappolas?" he asked. "Would you like for me to have your secretary join us?"

"Thank you, Mr. Deaton, but I'll be fine once the shock passes." Nicholas smiled thinly, a hint of color beginning to return to his face. He glanced down at the report, then back to Ian.

185

"You're a very clever man, Mr. Deaton. Very clever."

Ian didn't pretend ignorance. He knew exactly what Nicholas was talking about. "I've made a career of dealing with individuals, Mr. Pappolas. There've been times when—in the course of my work—I've found myself ashamed of the human race and the cruelties so-called 'people' inflict upon the weaker of their brethren. I decided early on in my career to try to instill some sort of protective shield around the innocents who became involved with my cases."

"And that's why you haven't identified my . . . my child?" Nicholas asked quietly.

"Precisely," Ian replied, not flinching or backing down one iota. "I'm not trying to play God, but you must understand that we're operating under the assumption that this person has never heard of you. In all good conscience I couldn't let you barge into someone's life and possibly destroy that person."

"Your advice wasn't part of the contract, Mr. Deaton," Nicholas said concisely and coolly. "Are you by any chance attempting to blackmail me?"

Ian smiled. "Rest assured, Mr. Pappolas, the fee we agreed on is quite sufficient. Call it the conscientious meddling of an old fool."

"I could take you to court."

"You could, but I don't think for one minute

you will. You're an honorable man, Nicholas Pappolas. Your child should be honored to claim you as a father. But"—Ian held up a pudgy hand—"that is a decision that child should be allowed to make alone. Or at least be allowed some privacy in which to get to know you. Don't you agree?"

"Certainly." Nicholas nodded.

Ian grinned. "I'm glad we understand each other."

"I hope you understand that a man in my position has to examine an issue from all angles. I had to be sure you were the man I thought you to be."

"No harm done. So." Ian eased his plump body to the edge of the chair. "I feel I have one more duty before I complete this case. I would deem it an honor if you would allow me to accompany you on a small trip. This is one of those rare cases where I can almost predict the outcome as being a happy one."

"How small a trip?" Nicholas asked, striving to keep some measure of control over the happiness building up within him.

"Arizona."

"I'd be happy for you to accompany me, Mr. Deaton." Nicholas grinned, and Ian Deaton saw in him something of what the Greek must have looked like as a younger man. "But only if you're prepared to leave within the hour."

"So long?" Ian asked innocently. "I took the

liberty of stashing my bag with your secretary. I was hoping you would allow me to see this through to the end."

Both men stood. Nicholas leaned across the desk and extended his hand. "Thank you, Ian. I admire a man with integrity."

CHAPTER ELEVEN

The next day, while stopping by her apartment for a quick sandwich, Shay heard a knock at the door. She opened it to find her roommate, looking slightly nervous.

"Becky!" she exclaimed, quickly reaching for her friend's arm and drawing her into the living room. "I was hoping you'd get back today."

"Wow!" Becky murmured as she ran an appreciative eye over the modular, glass-topped tables and geometric fabric designs on the sofa and chairs. "This is fantastic. But the house." She turned back to Shay, her expression full of sympathy. "That must have been awful. I'm sorry."

"I know." Shay nodded. "Everyone's been super. The workmen I hired started this morning, so hopefully, we—I'll be settled back in before too much longer."

"Well . . ." Becky glanced around. "I'm sure it's more convenient for you at the house, but this is certainly more sophisticated. I love it."

"Really?" Shay wrinkled her nose. "I don't. It's too modern for me. Each time I enter this room, I feel as if I'm on a spaceship. At any rate, since you were going to be leaving in a few days, I only took a one-bedroom. I hope you don't mind sharing for a few nights."

"Of course not," Becky assured her. "But we might get to share for at least two weeks more. The girl I'll be replacing in the New York office won't be leaving her position for another three weeks." She grimaced. "Big business cares little for the poor working stiffs whose lives they disrupt by the decisions they seem to pull out of thin air."

"I agree." Shay smiled. "But in this particular instance I can't really complain. With an extra week or two we'll have time for a couple of parties. Come on and let me show you the rest of the place."

After Becky was settled and had eaten a sandwich with Shay, they sat around the table chatting. Each caught the other up on their activities during the other's absence. Becky confessed that she hoped she wouldn't have to spend too many more months going from one part of the globe to the other. She'd met a man and was really interested in him. He seemed to return her feelings, and she was hopeful.

"I'm glad," Shay said softly. "I hate to sound

trite, but everybody needs somebody, don't they?"

"How is the battle getting on with Kurt?" Becky asked, recognizing the signs of unhappiness in her friend.

"Just that, a battle."

"You really love him, don't you?"

"You know something, Becky, I've only just discovered that I do," Shay confessed shyly. "For years I've worshiped him. Everybody who's ever known me knows that Kurt Barron has always been my idol. Then suddenly, a few months ago, something changed." She ducked her head in embarrassment. "I found myself getting angry when I knew he'd been out with some woman. I began resenting him treating me either like an old, comfortable shoe or a three-year-old. When I finally worked out my feelings and decided that my adoration had grown into a mature love of a woman for a man, I was floored. I still haven't completely recovered."

Becky laughed at the comical, yet touching, predicament her roommate found herself in.

"It isn't funny in the least, I can assure you." Shay grinned ruefully.

"I know, it's just that the two of you are so perfect for each other. And from the few months I've been around you, I seriously doubt any of your other friends will be at all surprised if the two of you become an item."

"Oh, great." Shay moaned, hiding her face for a moment behind her hands. "Loving someone is one thing. Having the entire world smirking and more than likely making wagers on the outcome behind your back is something else."

By the time Shay left the apartment to return to the greenhouse, she was absolutely disgusted with herself and her wishy-washy attitude where Kurt was concerned.

She frowned as she drove along. Last night she'd been positive she wanted him, and the light of day hadn't changed her mind. Letting him know her feelings had seemed the obvious thing to do. Today, however, she wondered if she'd made the correct move. Kurt was a wily adversary, one who was just as determined *not* to give in to his real feelings as she was that he do so.

Of course, she reasoned, another possibility could be that he didn't care for her.

No, she didn't want to believe such an outrageous thing. She'd spent a lifetime "Kurtwatching." She probably knew as much about him as he did himself. He had been her favorite subject for as long as she could remember.

But what if? . . . What if?

"Then, dammit, I'll face it," she muttered in a fierce undertone. But deep in her heart, she knew that if such a thing were to happen, it would quite likely destroy her.

She pulled into the driveway and drove the van at a snail's pace till she reached the greenhouse. The moment she unlocked the door, the telephone began ringing. Shay rushed forward, dropping her purse and a couple of trade magazines on her worktable as she grabbed up the receiver. "Hello?"

"Shay? Ted, over at the lab. Got a minute?"

"Sure thing, Ted. How's it going?" Shay relaxed against the edge of the thick plywood surface that served as one of her three worktops. Ted Hemeter was a nice guy and she always enjoyed talking to him. His lab always gave prompt service, and Shay used him exclusively for soil samples as an aid in creating the correct pH balance for most of the larger displays she used.

"First of all, I want to know who's playing a trick on who?" he surprised her by asking.

"Trick? What on earth are you talking about?"

"These soil samples you sent me." He laughed. "Damndest thing I've ever seen."

"If you'd only clue me in," Shay told him, "perhaps I could share your amusement."

"Bourbon, honey. Plain ole eighty- or ninety-proof bourbon. Those damned soil samples were so potent I almost got soused just testing them."

"You're kidding!"

"Not in the least. I'd say at least a gallon or better had been dumped in the planter."

"Turn the heat on at night," she remarked in a barely audible voice, "and you could kill a stand of aspens."

"What was that, Shay?"

"Er . . . nothing of importance, Ted. I was just thinking out loud. Listen, I can't imagine who on earth would do such a terrible thing. It's going to cost the owner a small fortune to replace everything. I'll pass on the information you've given me. Thanks a lot, Ted."

"Sure thing, Shay. See ya."

Shay stood staring into space, a combination of anger and uncertainty plaguing her. Was Kurt the culprit? she asked. Of course he was, she quickly concluded. Why on earth would he deliberately destroy such an expensive and beautiful array of plants? Had he been trying to get back at her?

She thought back to the morning she'd gone rushing over to personally see the damage. Kurt had been friendly, she remembered. He'd even insisted they share a cool drink. As a matter of fact—Shay's eyes narrowed in speculation—that fink hadn't been unduly concerned at all.

Without giving herself time to change her mind, she reached for the phone and dialed Kurt's office. When the Golden Throat of the

West answered, Shay felt her hackles rise. She detested the damn woman.

"This is Shay Michaels. I'd like to speak with Mr. Barron, please."

"One moment, Ms. Michaels, while I see if Mr. Barron is available."

"Tell him he'd better be available, Ms. Gray. Oh . . . by the way. That's a threat."

"Well, really, Ms. Michaels. I can't imagine what Mr. Barron will say to that."

"Don't strain yourself, just deliver the message."

Seconds later Kurt was on the line. "Something wrong, Shay?" he quickly asked, the note of concern unnoticed by Shay as she nurtured her anger against him for killing her lovely plants.

"Bourbon is what's wrong, Kurtland. I got a report on the soil samples taken from your planter, you lying dog," she informed him in a low, furious voice.

"Er . . . Shay . . . honey, I can explain," he stumbled, not even bothering to defend himself against the charges. He'd known this moment was coming, but somewhere in the back of his mind, he hadn't expected it quite so soon.

"I'm listening."

"Not now. Not while you're mad. Have dinner with me this evening," Kurt suggested trying for the diplomatic approach. "You're a reasonable person, sweetheart. I know that as soon as you hear my side of the story, you'll understand perfectly."

"People in hell want ice water, Kurt."

"I beg your pardon?"

"You heard me. That's about as close to getting me to understand your doing such a thing as you'll get. I cannot begin to understand why a man of your intelligence and wealth would skulk around like some wimp and douse his plants with bourbon. You need help," she threw at him, then slammed down the receiver.

Moments later the phone rang. But instead of answering, Shay waited for her answering machine to take the message. In a matter of seconds she heard Kurt.

"Shay, sweetheart," he began. "I'll be by at six-thirty to take you out to dinner. I won't take no for an answer."

"Don't worry." Shay grinned evilly. "I wouldn't miss it for the world." She picked up her purse and keys, then turned and headed for the front door of the greenhouse. It was time she had a long chat with Jane.

Several minutes later Jane Corley opened the door, a look of surprise on her attractive face. "Oh, my." She smiled. "I do feel honored. You never take time off during the day to visit me." Suddenly the smile was wiped from her face, replaced with concern. "You're pregnant."

Shay stared at her sister as she'd suddenly gone stark, raving mad. "Can you tell that just by looking into my face? Christ! That ought to prove interesting. Frankly, I thought you had to kill a rabbit or something, Janey."

"Don't do this to me," Jane said sternly. She caught Shay's arm and pulled her inside, then slammed the door. "So are you pregnant?" she asked pointedly.

"Of course not," she murmured. "Well, probably not."

"What does Kurt say on the subject?"

"What subject? Rabbits?"

"Nooo," Jane wailed, "pregnancy and marriage."

"Why, I don't know," Shay told her. "We haven't discussed pregnancy, only marriage."

"How wonderful," Jane enthused. She slipped an arm around Shay's waist, the impetus of her enthusiasm carrying them to the kitchen, where Jane had apparently been working when Shay arrived. "Have a seat and I'll cut you a piece of coconut cake. Coffee?"

"Please."

"Oh, I just love weddings. What date did you come up with?"

"I haven't decided yet."

"But I thought you said you and Kurt had discussed it."

"Actually," Shay hedged, "I did most of the talking on the subject."

"I see," Jane said slowly, comprehension beginning to dawn. She placed coffee and cake for each of them on the table, then sat down opposite Shay. "Honey, do you think maybe you're going about this thing all wrong? I mean, I know you love Kurt . . . now, at this moment. But will you still love him next week, next month?"

"You sound exactly like Kurt, Jane," Shay frowned darkly. "You've both protected me so long, it's a wonder I'm allowed out without a keeper."

"That's not so, honey. It's just"—she shook her head—"I just want you to be sure."

"Sure?" Shay repeated. "How can anyone be sure about anything, Janey? Can you assure me that if I wait till I'm thirty years old to marry Kurt, we'll be deliriously happy?"

"Of course not."

"Then I rest my case. Now. How would you like to help me work on Kurt's and my wedding announcement? I want to get it finished this afternoon so that I can show it to Kurt this evening at dinner."

"Your what?" Jane cried, her eyes big as saucers. It was one thing for her baby sister deliberately to antagonize Kurt, but Jane wasn't so certain she wanted to share the "rewards."

198

* * *

The moment Shay opened the door to Kurt, she could see that he was in his most conciliatory mood. That alone set her teeth on edge, and had her ready to fight on the spot. She was dressed in a brilliant-orange dress with a plunging neckline that almost hit her navel! It was new, bought after she'd left Jane's house, and Shay knew without a doubt that it was the most uncomfortable dress she'd ever worn. She planned to burn it as soon as the evening was over.

"You look charming," he said in his most seductive voice, his wide hands clasping her shoulders as he bent and slowly brushed his lips against hers.

Shay stepped back from his embrace, struggling to stem the flame of desire unfolding within her at his touch. He was a dishonorable pig. "The last time you saw me in a dress this revealing," she said coolly, "you informed me that I looked like a woman on the make. Remember?"

"So I did." Kurt nodded. Frankly, he told himself, he hadn't liked her showing so much cleavage then and he didn't like it now. However, since he found himself in hot water over the plants, he'd let the matter of her dress wait. "I've changed my mind," he offered placatingly. "My remarks that evening were rude. I apologize."

Shay regarded him suspiciously. "That's a crock, and you know it. Anything short of a granny collar around my neck almost gives you hives. I haven't forgotten the first time you caught me in a bikini. You almost had a heart attack."

"Hell, yes," Kurt threw back at her, momentarily forgetting his resolve to atone for harming her spathaphylum . . . or whatever the hell she called the thing. "The occasion was you entertaining a whole platoon of boys in my pool with nothing covering your body but two narrow strips of red cloth."

"The occasion," she said stingingly, "was a party, which you'd given me permission to have around your pool. When you first saw me and almost passed out, the first three guests had arrived. They were boys. By the time the others got there, we were pretty evenly paired off."

She picked up her off-white, lace stole and slipped it over her shoulders, her small clutch in one hand. "Shall we go?"

Kurt gritted his teeth as he escorted her to the car, then got behind the wheel and drove off. This whole scenario was getting out of hand. This evening was it. It would be over. Finished. As painful as it was, he had decided the best thing for him to do was stop seeing Shay.

No matter what it took, he would do it. So

far, she'd interfered with his sleep, he wasn't eating properly, his mind wandered during important business conferences, and he couldn't concentrate on a damned thing. All he thought about these days was the irritating little witch sitting like a pouting kitten beside him, and how incredibly wonderful it was to make love to her.

"Would you mind telling me where we're having dinner?" Shay asked, breaking the tense silence.

Kurt named a well-established restaurant with entertainment and dancing. Shay had been there a number of times and she liked it. She said as much to Kurt.

"Is that where you spend your evenings with Wes?" he asked curtly.

"On occasion. And you? Are you a frequent visitor?"

"On occasion," he parroted.

So much for an attempt at civil conversation, Shay told herself. She sat rigidly, as close to the door as she could possibly get, till they arrived at the restaurant.

When they were shown to a choice table with the subtle deference to which Kurt was accustomed, Shay looked at him accusingly the minute they were seated and alone. "Now I know what you mean when you say 'on occasion,' don't I?"

"What's that supposed to mean?" he

snapped. Not even a measly thirty minutes had elapsed since he'd arrived at her door, and already he was mad as hell! A body couldn't stand this constant irritation, Kurt kept lecturing himself. Simply couldn't stand it.

"Well," Shay answered with a shrug, "it's obvious from the gushy way you were treated that you're practically a fixture here. Why did you pour that damned bourbon on my plants?" she demanded in the same breath just as a youngish waiter materialized at their table.

"I wanted to annoy the hell out of you," he retorted as he snatched the menus from the startled waiter's hand, then thrust one at Shay. "They're having barbecued rattlesnake this evening at my request . . . just for you. Order it, it should improve your personality."

Shay bit her lip to keep from telling him exactly where he could go, and what he could do with his rattlesnake. She made her decision, closed the menu, then smiled so sweetly at the clearly rattled young man, his mouth dropped open. "I'll have three Margaritas, one at a time, of course, with double tequila."

The waiter turned regretfully to a scowling Kurt, who was regarding him like a tiger ready to pounce. "And you, sir?"

"Scotch on the rocks," he snapped. "And a pot of coffee."

Shay flushed at the blatant implication that she would be needing the "sobering" effect of the coffee. She leaned forward. "Can't you hold your liquor?"

Before she could sit back, Kurt's hand snaked across the table, his forefinger pressed against her lips. To the casual onlooker it looked as if they were two lovers, exchanging a moment of tenderness. But not so Shay, for she alone could see the dangerous glitter of anger reflected in his eyes.

"Don't say another word," Kurt said warningly, his voice low and threatening. He removed his finger, then caught her hand toying with her water glass. "We've done nothing from the moment you opened your door but trade insults. The only time we don't argue is when we're making love."

Shay opened her mouth to send him a zinger of a reply, then stopped. What he'd said was true, she silently acknowledged. Her gaze dropped to the snowy linen cloth covering the table. How had their relationship gotten so far off track that it could be turned into a continuous brawl?

"I'm sorry," she said barely above a whisper. "I honestly don't know why I've been so bitchy lately."

"I don't want an apology, honey." Kurt's gruff response sent a rush of warmth stealing over her. "I just want us to be able to enjoy ourselves this evening. Why don't you tell me how long the workmen think it will be before you can return to your house?"

Shay did, and with each word that passed between them, the tension lessened and they relaxed. The waiter returned with their drinks, and soon the topic of conversation went from the repair of her house to the shopping center Kurt was building, the fact that he was presently her landlord, and several other projects he had invested heavily in. When the stock market came up, he looked astonished when he learned Shay owned some rather nice stocks.

"Surprised?" She smiled.

"Yes, I am. On the other hand I don't know why," he remarked. "Hardly a day goes by that I don't learn something new or different about you. Just out of curiosity, who advised you on the stock?" There was an underlying trace of jealousy in his voice that wasn't lost on Shay.

"Wes Pollock. He's a broker, remember?"

"Ahh, yes, the ever-handy Wes."

Shay gave him a look of mock sternness. "No, no," she teased. "You were the instigator of this particular evening's peace treaty, and you will darn well stick to the bargain. There'll be no more remarks about Wes, and I won't even bother to mention that I'm almost positive Tessa has had a face-lift. See how fair I can be?"

Kurt almost choked on his Scotch, his amusement getting the best of him. She was without a doubt the most delightful creature he'd ever known. None of the other women he knew could hold a candle to her when it came to making him laugh. But then, he mused as he watched her raise the Margarita to her lips, neither could any of the other women make him as furious.

"Why are you staring at me like a huge cat stalking a canary?" she demanded.

"What if I were to say it's because you look exceptionally beautiful this evening . . . in spite of the dress"—his gaze lingering on the quite visible swell of her breasts—"and that I find you very . . . er . . . stimulating to be with."

"Physically or intellectually?"

"Both." Kurt grinned. "Definitely both."

"Oooh," Shay said softly, "I do appreciate a diplomatic gentleman, Mr. Barron."

The waiter came back for their order, then faded from their sight again. They talked and laughed and argued good-naturedly. Shay knew it was a rare moment, a milestone in their relationship. Kurt was seeing her as a woman who could think about such things as investments, world trouble spots, and the mystique of the Los Angeles Raiders, of whom she was a devoted fan.

Shay couldn't help but wonder, during one brief but companionable lull in the conversation, how Kurt would view the slip of paper in her purse, on which she'd written—with Jane's help—the announcement of their engagement. She even wondered if she should give it to him this evening. Since they hadn't argued from the time they'd ordered their drinks, and Kurt hadn't reverted back to his old self, maybe she wouldn't need the announcement after all.

Kurt and Shay were so caught up in the thoughts of congratulating themselves on the success of their date, neither of them noticed the two middle-aged men who were shown to a table on the opposite side of the dining room. At first the shorter, portly member of the duo cast a cursory glance around the room, looked down at the menu, then quickly back to where Kurt and Shay were sitting.

Ian Deaton debated only a second before coming to a decision. "Nicholas? Are you ready for the shock of your life?" he asked in a controlled voice.

Nicholas Pappolas stared at the detective, his strong features growing taut as leather. "Life's a shock at times, Ian. Let's have it."

"If you'll look to your right, at the table where the young woman is wearing the red dress, you'll see your child."

Nicholas's head swung almost drunkenly to the right, his hands going to the arms of the chair he was sitting in and clutching the polished wood in a death grip. He saw the lovely girl first, then let his eyes go to the commanding figure of the man, a man who looked to be as tall as Nicholas. It was difficult trying to figure out the ages of either, due to the dim lighting in the restaurant.

Out of the Pappolas pride racing through his veins at the moment, Nicholas's lips curved into a smile of possession. Already he could see those wide shoulders across the room assuming the mantle of responsibility for Pappolas Shipping. His entire body appeared to sag with relief. He turned back to Ian Deaton, humility and gratefulness showing in his gaze. "You don't have to tell me." And then he smiled. "That has to be my son. His hair looks as dark as mine used to be, and he's every bit as tall as I am."

"Yes." Ian nodded pleasantly. "He's all those things, isn't he? But look again, my friend."

Nicholas turned back, wondering what Ian was referring to.

"I didn't find you a son, Nicholas. I found you a daughter. Miss Shay Michaels, to be precise."

CHAPTER TWELVE

Nicholas could feel his mouth drop open, but it seemed an interminable length of time before he could do anything about it.

"That beautiful creature sitting over there is my daughter?" he asked, his astonishment so real, Ian Deaton grinned.

"She is the daughter of Emily Crawford Michaels. Your daughter Shay was born approximately seven and one half months after the death of John Crawford."

"Then Emily did remarry," Nicholas said quietly, his mind literally buzzing with so many facts and dates.

"Not necessarily," Ian told him. "A person has the right to change her name, you know. Emily did this when Shay was approximately six weeks old. The records will verify that. As to Shay being your daughter, John Crawford was in a coma for months and months before he finally died. There was no medical or physical way on earth he could have fathered a child.

And unless you think there was another man involved, I believe it's safe to say that the young lady sitting over there is your daughter. There's one other thing, Nicholas."

"What's that?" a dazed Nicholas asked.

"She has a sister. A few years older than herself. The two are very close. It's my own opinion, of course"—Ian tipped his head forward—"but if I were you, I think you'd better be prepared to make room in your heart for two daughters instead of one. Jane, that's the older one, is married to a dentist. Their little girl is three years old."

Ian motioned for the waiter. When he arrived, the detective ordered double bourbon and water for both Nicholas and himself. He sat back then, and shrewdly regarded his client. "Well? You thought you had a boy. Are you disappointed to learn that it's a girl instead?"

"No!" Nicholas was emphatic. "Boy, girl, I don't care which, just as long as I know. But now that that problem's settled, how the hell do I go about getting to know her?"

"Well . . ." Ian leaned forward, remaining silent till the departure of the waiter who had brought their drinks. "As I was saying," he went on, "I think you should work this thing through the man she's with. You might know him if you were to get a good look at his face."

"Oh?"

"Yes. Name's Kurt Barron."

"I've heard of him." Nicholas nodded, surprised.

"Well, here in this part of the country he's considered pretty important. He's a millionaire, has his finger in just about everything there is that makes money, and is a bachelor to boot. Seems he's lived next door to Shay and her family since Shay was knee high to a grasshopper. From what I could tell, they're pretty close."

Nicholas didn't like the sound of that at all. Some bizarre male pride came rushing to the surface of his being, making him jealous of any other man in his daughter's life. He'd only just found her. Couldn't the gods allow him even a few months, a few years, with her?

For a moment he pinned Kurt's profile with a cold blue stare, then let his gaze slide to Shay. He tried the name and found he liked the way it sounded. Suddenly he wanted to get up and go over to her table and tell her who he was. But perhaps Deaton was right. He sighed. There were the feelings of more people to consider than just his own.

"Would you like to go somewhere else and eat?" Ian asked, bringing Nicholas out of his thoughtful reverie.

"What?" Nicholas turned and stared at the other man and at the waiter, who was ready to take their order. "Oh. Sorry, I didn't mean to hold up our dinner." He gave his order, barely aware of what he was saying, then resumed watching each and every move Shay made.

The steady scrutiny she was being subjected to finally registered with Shay. At first she tried to ignore it, giving her full attention to Kurt. But when the tall, distinguished gentleman made no effort to hide the fact that he was watching her, Shay became uneasy.

"That man is making me nervous," she murmured as she took the last bite of her dessert, then touched her napkin to her mouth.

"What man?" Kurt asked. He'd already finished and was having a brandy and Benedictine.

"Look to your left. There are two men sitting at a table across the room. The tall one hasn't taken his eyes off me since they came in."

Instead of looking, Kurt made as if to get up. Shay grabbed at his arm. "What on earth are you doing?" she hissed.

"You're going to point out the table to me, then I'm going to walk over and ask the man to stop staring at you. If he doesn't choose to do so, then I'll invite him outside for a little chat. Why?"

"Don't you dare!" she said crossly. "Everything you do makes the papers. Can you imagine the hullabaloo there'd be if some reporter were to get wind of something like this? They'd have you involved in a barroom brawl before you could blink your eyes. Let's just leave."

But as they were making their way past one particular table, Nicholas Pappolas rose to his feet. Shay glared at him, not in the least impressed with his good looks.

"Mr. Barron?" Nicholas nodded to Kurt and extended his hand. "My name is Nicholas Pappolas."

"I know," Kurt replied as he shook hands. He'd recognized the shipping tycoon the moment he set eyes on him. He nodded to Ian Deaton, then turned back to the tall man blocking their way and who was still staring at Shay.

Kurt slipped a protective arm around Shay's waist and pulled her close to his side. "What brings you to Flagstaff, Mr. Pappolas?" he asked coolly. No wonder Shay had been edgy, he reflected with a frown. The damned man looked ready to gobble her up on the spot.

"Business. Mr. Barron, would it be possible for me to make an appointment with you for . . . say nine o'clock in the morning?"

"Nine o'clock will be fine," Kurt told him.

Kurt escorted Shay out of the restaurant, and Nicholas got the distinct impression that if he hadn't moved out of the way, the younger man would have knocked him flat on his behind.

"Well?" Ian asked once Nicholas was seated.

"Now I know what it means when someone

says he felt as if he were in a trance. I'm afraid if I blink my eyes it will all be gone."

"It's for real," Ian assured him. "Do you plan on taking Barron into your confidence?"

Nicholas chuckled. "Don't you think I'd better? I seriously doubt he would think twice about knocking me on my keister. And as for my daughter . . ." He smiled. "She looked ready to cave my head in with a poker. I wish I had my mother's picture with me, Ian. My daughter looks exactly as her grandmother did in her younger days. There is one thing you haven't mentioned. Did you find Emily?"

Ian rubbed the tip of one plump finger around the rim of his water glass. "Sorry, Nicholas. Emily died several years ago. She bought a small house from Barron's uncle when Shay was a baby. That's where she lived till she died. She never remarried."

"I see," Nicholas said softly, having no recourse but to admit finally that his Emily was well and truly beyond his reach. She'd wanted anonymity . . . he only hoped it had brought her happiness.

"Did I tell you that Becky got in today?" Shay asked as Kurt helped her out of the car at her apartment. "She's also learned that it will be at least another two weeks before she's to be in New York."

"Why didn't you tell me earlier that she was

home?" Kurt asked. "We could have gone to my place instead."

"Why should we have gone to your place?" she asked innocently, fitting without protest into the curve of his body as he pulled her into his arms.

"Because I want to make love to you." His mouth covered hers, and Shay felt as if she'd suddenly been flung off a cliff. She clung to him, her response as natural as the wind. The tiny groans of pleasure coming from deep within Kurt's throat created minute rivers of flaming need in Shay's veins. She loved him, and his touch, the scent of him, even the thought of him, left her trembling with the need for him to possess her.

"But not in the parking lot." The words were jarring, cutting like a metal edge through the silky illusion surrounding them. Kurt held her face between his palms, and touched his lips to her eyes and the tip of her nose. "Something had got to be done about this . . . and soon." He sighed roughly.

Shay smiled, almost feeling sorry for the poor, sweet dear. "Don't worry," she whispered. "Everything's going to work out just the way we want it to."

"The way you want it to, you mean." He scowled. Damn her! Kurt was thinking. He could feel the noose tightening around his

214

neck already. He had to take a stand. He absolutely, unequivocally refused to marry.

"Whatever," Shay said soothingly. She caught his arm and began walking toward her apartment. "Let's continue our discussion inside. Okay?"

"Sure." Kurt grunted, the easy rapport that had sprung up between them in the restaurant vanishing as he realized just how easily it had become for Shay to manipulate him. "I'm curious about something," he said as they walked along. "Why didn't you move into my house after the fire? There's plenty of room, and it would make things handier all around."

"You making love to me is one thing, Kurt," he was told in a calm voice. "But openly living with you is something else. I don't think I could handle a relationship like that."

"But you could live with me if we were married?" he asked mockingly.

Shay pulled at her bottom lip with her teeth as she thought over the remark. "There are moments when I think it would be wonderful being married to you. And then there are times, such as this very second, when I wouldn't touch you with a ten-foot pole."

He caught her arm and swung her around to face him. "What the hell's that suppose to mean?" he said roughly.

"Just returning nasty for nasty." She glared

at him. "I don't care to be *handy* for anyone, including you. Is that understood?"

"I'm sorry," he muttered. "It was a cheap shot."

"Why did you feel you needed to say something like that?" she asked curiously. So far, Shay thought, the entire evening had been like a crash course in learning and understanding new and different aspects of Kurt's personality.

One long arm slipped behind her waist, while the other hand caught her chin. "You've stirred my world into a swirling mass of confusion, honey." He grinned down at her. "We're both determined people. The outcome should prove interesting."

"You will forgive me if I don't feel the slightest bit of sympathy for you, won't you?" Shay laughed. She paused at her door and handed him the key.

"Heartless wench."

"That's because I was taught not to trust men by my guardian angel when I was very young." When he opened the door, she swept by him with her nose in the air.

"Your guardian angel has a damned loose screw. All the things he taught you, are now being used against him. It's called blackmail, you know." There was a loud crash, then another, as they both stumbled into things. "For Christ's sake, Shay, turn on a light."

"Is your arm broken?" she asked.

216

Kurt muttered an especially ugly retort while he was fumbling around for the light switch. "Hell's bell's! What's happened here?" he exclaimed the moment the light came on.

The room looked as if a cyclone had gone through it. Shay stood rooted to the spot, unable to take in the complete chaos surrounding her. "I don't believe this," she said in a voice barely above a whisper. She began picking up cushions and placing them on the sofa, then reached for a lamp.

"I think you should wait, honey," Kurt warned her as he came back into the room after a quick survey of the bath and bedroom. "It's the same in there. The police will want to get some prints."

"Prints of what?"

"Fingerprints, Shay. It looks like you've had a burglar."

Shay looked about her, then dropped down onto the sofa. "Frankly, Kurt, the last few weeks have been like something out of a horror film. I wrecked my van, some *ass*"—she glared meaningfully at him—"poured gallons of bourbon into a lovely setting of plants, my house burned, and now my apartment has been burgled. And the problem with this last little fiasco is, every damn thing is so jumbled up, I couldn't tell if anything was missing if I wanted to."

Kurt walked over and pulled her to her feet

and into his arms. He rested his chin against her hair while gently rocking her in his arms. "I'm sorry, sweetheart. Now that you mention it, it does look as if you've had more than your fair share of problems, doesn't it?"

Shay merely nodded, letting the warmth of him seep through her and quell the fear and anger consuming her. Knowing that some low-life had prowled at leisure through her personal things and those of Becky . . .

Becky!

"Oh, my God, Kurt! Where on earth is Becky?" she cried.

"I assumed she was out on a date."

"No." Shay shook her head. "She was going to do a little shopping and be home early. I won—"

At that moment the sound of a key sounded in the door. Kurt pushed Shay behind him, as they both swung around to face whoever it was entering the apartment.

"Becky! Thank goodness you're okay," Shay exclaimed. "Where have you been?" She started toward her roommate, when she noticed the bandage peeking out from beneath the edges of her hair. "What happened to your head?"

"I got back from shopping, took a shower, and was about to get my pajamas on. I stepped into the closet to hang up a couple of blouses. Just as I finished and was about to turn, someone hit me on the back of my head." She fingered the edge of the bandage. "I got this when I fell."

"Were you harmed in any other way, Becky?" Kurt asked the frightened girl.

"No." She shook her head. "Just the lick to my head. The neighbors have been nice enough to take care of me for the last hour, calm me down. I was so upset."

"Dear heavens," Shay murmured. "Come." She took Becky by the arm. "You'd better sit down. Kurt thinks we should call the police."

"I agree. I was just about to do that from next door when I heard the two of you in here."

"Why don't you change into something more comfortable?" Kurt said close to Shay's ear once he'd made the call, and Becky had left the room.

"This dress is comfortable," she said defiantly.

"Not to me, nor do I think the officers of the law will find it so. It reveals far too much, and what it does cover can cause the imagination to slam into orbit."

After that monologue on the "shortcomings" of her attire, Shay looked down curiously at the brilliant creation, clearly amused by Kurt's remarks. "Just to prove that I am constantly thinking of ways to keep you happy, I'll hurry and change clothes before we're surrounded by the constabulary."

Kurt grinned. "Thank you, Ms. Michaels. I'm delighted you see things my way for a change."

"Oh . . . don't let this one little victory go to your head, you obnoxious person." Shay frowned at him. "Tomorrow is a new day, and I still haven't forgiven you for destroying my plants."

Before she could guess his intentions, Kurt plucked her from the floor and lifted her till her face was on level with his. "I declared war on that damned jungle of greenery in order to get you over to my office," he confessed without a flicker of conscience.

"That's terrible."

"Not at all. You had gone around for days with your nose in the air, ignoring me. I didn't like that."

"I was ignoring you at your own suggestion," Shay countered.

"Then why did you choose that particular time to listen to me?" he teased. "You never have before."

Shay shook her head and sighed. "I give up. But there is one thing that still puzzles me. Did something happen to the air-conditioning or was that another of your little tricks?"

"I turned it off in the reception area, hoping the heat would help the bourbon along with making the plants ill."

"You're cruel." She leaned forward till her lips were pressing against his, the tip of her tongue teasing the outline of his mouth. Kurt groaned, then caught her head and held it still, his tongue plunging into her mouth and setting off a series of explosions rippling throughout her being. Shay was the first to cry for mercy. "Please—remember my dress."

Kurt's gaze was glued to the now gaping bodice, her breasts in plain view due to the way he was holding her. "I am remembering, honey, and it's damned near killing me." He set her on her feet and gave her a slap on the behind. "Hurry, our guests should be arriving any minute now."

The next hour and a half were taken over with the police, questions, and attempts to figure out why the apartment had been broken into. From what Shay and Becky could see, there didn't appear to be anything missing. That was even more baffling. It was beginning to look as though the wrong apartment had been broken into. It was suggested that perhaps it would be best if the girls could find someplace else to stay for a couple of days.

"We can bunk in with Jane till this mess is cleaned up," Shay argued once the authorities were gone and she was forced by Kurt to pack. She sought out Becky, hoping to find an ally. "What's your opinion? Do you want to stay with Kurt or go over to Jane's?"

"Kurt's got more room," Becky pointed out, unconsciously fingering the bandage on her

221

forehead. "On the other hand, I'll be leaving tomorrow for another three-day trip, so the decision of where to stay doesn't concern me nearly as much as you."

"The decision's already been made," Kurt spoke up. He took each girl's bag and headed for the door. "Let's get moving."

"Masterful men give me a pain in the behind," Shay muttered as she brought up the rear.

When they reached Kurt's house, he showed Becky to one of the guest rooms with its own connecting bath. Shay, who was still trailing behind, looked expectantly at him as he closed the door to Becky's room.

"Which one can I use?"

"The last one on the right."

She turned and stared down the length of the hall. "That's at least half a mile away. Besides"—she turned back to him, a suspicious look on her face—"isn't that your room?"

"My, you're smart tonight." Kurt chuckled. He picked up her suitcase, caught her arm in a firm grip, and hustled her down the hall to his bedroom, humming all the way.

"Are you quite sure you didn't torch my house and hire someone to scare us into leaving the apartment?"

"I'm sorry to say I didn't think of that, but I'll keep it in mind for future use." He dropped the case by the closet, then indicated the huge master bath. "I think you know where most everything is, but if you need anything you can just whisper, I'll hear you."

Shay let forth with a rather indelicate hoot of derision. "You do realize, don't you, that you've done a complete hundred-and-eighty-degree turn?"

"Females aren't the only ones allowed to change their mind," she was shortly informed.

"I can see that." She walked over to the other side of the bed and helped him fold back the large hand-woven throw he used as a spread. It was one of many of the Indian pieces scattered throughout the old house. "What made you change your mind?" she asked out of curiosity.

"Responsibility," he replied with feigned innocence. "What other reason could there be?"

"What other reason, indeed?" she snapped. She stalked over to where her case was, got out a nightgown and her makeup kit, then stormed into the bathroom. When she came out, there was no sign of Kurt. Shay turned off the light and went to bed. Nerves and exhaustion made her a prisoner of sleep almost immediately.

At some point during the night she woke up enough to be aware of an incredible feeling of warmth from her feet to her head. It felt as if a giant heating pad had been permanently attached to her back. She wiggled around till her face was against a hairy roughness, and a large hand was lightly stroking her from her shoulders to her hips. His touch brought an instant response from Shay, and before she slept again they made love.

CHAPTER THIRTEEN

There was contempt written in Phillip Norcross's face as he stared at the individual seated
across from him. "You did not complete the
job, Hunter."

"You hired me to create a certain atmo-
sphere. That's all you paid me to do," the man
named Hunter said harshly. There was an iciness in his eyes that caused one to want to
finish one's business with him as quickly as possible and get on one's way. His skin had an
unhealthy pallor, and Phillip had never been
more uncomfortable in his life than he was at
this precise moment.

"I changed my mind and instructed you to
get rid of the problem."

"You wanted me to wipe out someone, Norcross. That's what you're afraid to say. Let's get
one thing straight now. I don't take orders over
the telephone, then wait for my money to
come later. In my business it isn't very smart
working on credit. We made a deal, I carried

out my end of the bargain. Now our business is complete." He pushed back his chair and started to get to his feet.

"Okay," Phillip said hastily. "Please . . . let's talk. I . . . er . . . there's someone—"

"Give me a name, an address, and half my fee now. I'll collect the rest when the job is done." He named an amount that caused Phillip to swallow hastily. Seeing his reaction, Hunter gave a humorless chuckle. "It's not as though I was going to the supermarket for a head of cabbage, you know."

"No . . . er . . . no, I suppose not," Phillip replied nervously. He sat forward, then removed a slip of paper from his inside jacket pocket, along with a photograph. "Why don't you ask any other questions you need to and I'll try to answer them for you."

Hunter snorted disgustedly. "Let's start off by giving me the information."

Kurt was just completing a telephone conversation the next morning when his secretary, Colleen Gray, came in to let him know that the most "charming gentleman" was waiting to see him, a Mr. Pappolas.

"Hmmm," Kurt murmured, glancing at his watch. He honestly hadn't expected the man to keep the appointment, thinking the attempt at conversation the evening before had been

Pappolas's ploy to get himself introduced to Shay.

Kurt's blood boiled at even the thought of the man touching Shay. "Send him in. And, Colleen—"

"Yes, Mr. Barron," she gushed, an affectation that had her boss ready to climb the walls.

"Buzz me in thirty minutes. I have more important things to do than sit all morning chatting with some wealthy Greek."

"Certainly, Mr. Barron." She smiled, then announced Nicholas.

"Mr. Barron." Nicholas smiled pleasantly as he entered the office. He walked straight to Kurt's desk and extended his hand.

For a second Kurt was tempted to ignore the gesture, but he didn't. He hadn't liked this "much older" man making for Shay. Nicholas noticed that brief pause, and all but laughed. So, he mused, Barron still had his nose out of joint over last night. At least his daughter had a man who was willing to look out for her interests. That pleased Nicholas.

"Please." Kurt waved to a chair in front of the desk. "Have a seat." He looked expectantly at his guest. "What can I do for you?"

"Quite a lot, I hope."

Kurt frowned. "Would you be more specific?"

"May I call you Kurt?" Nicholas surprised him by asking.

"Of course."

"Good. You'll call me Nicholas. Now that we've got that out of the way, I'll try to explain. Please try to be patient with me, this is a very difficult story to recount. Several years ago, Kurt, in fact, many years ago, I met and fell in love with a lovely woman . . . a married woman. We became involved in an affair and I began to suspect that she was pregnant with my child. Unfortunately, I voiced my suspicions regarding her pregnancy and the lady panicked. She chose to sever our relationship without apprising me of her intention to do so, and quite naturally I was angry when I discovered that she was gone. After my anger cooled down, I tried to find her but to no avail. I wanted her, but if that wasn't to be, then I at least wanted to know my child. I have since learned that during the time shortly after she ran away from me, her husband, who had been seriously injured in an auto accident and remained comatose, died."

"Emily—that was her name," Nicholas briefly explained, "—sold their home, picked up her small daughter, and left. She deliberately covered her tracks, and managed to keep her whereabouts well hidden. Approximately three months ago I became ill and required back surgery. During that time I began to think of Emily, but mainly of my child. I didn't know if it was a boy or a girl . . . nor did I care. But I found it imperative that I *know* if I had a child. It began to prey on my mind. Finally, during my recuperation at my home in Connecticut, I decided to try once more to find her. I hired the best private detective and told him the story. Yesterday, that same detective brought me the results I've been hoping for. I have a daughter, and that daughter lives right here in Flagstaff."

For several long moments Kurt was silent. Christ! What did one say to a story like he'd just heard, he asked himself. And how on earth did it involve him? However, it was obvious the man was pleased with the outcome, so Kurt smiled cordially. "I'm sure you're very happy, Nicholas. But how do I figure into any of this?"

"I've been led to believe that you are very close to my daughter, Kurt. In fact"—Nicholas smiled—"you took her to dinner last night."

"I'm afraid you're mistaken, sir." Damnation. What kind of slime would feed the poor man that kind of story? "I took Shay Michaels to dinner. The same Shay Michaels I've known since she was a toddler, along with her mother, Suzanne Michaels, and Shay's sister, Jane. Suzanne bought a small, three-bedroom house from my late uncle. Around the turn of the century it was used as servants' quarters and is situated to the right of the main house. Shay and Jane grew up there, and Suzanne remained there till her death a few years ago."

Kurt shook his head. "I'm sorry, but I'm afraid you've been given the wrong information."

Nicholas removed a faded, but still quite distinguishable, photograph from his inside jacket pocket and handed it across the desk to Kurt. "Do you recognize this woman?"

Kurt took the photograph. His first glance at the smiling woman was something of a shock. He'd never seen Emily Michaels with such a happy expression on her face. She was positively radiant. He looked sharply at Nicholas. "We knew her as Suzanne."

"Emily Suzanne was her full name," Nicholas supplied. "Jane was approximately three years old when I knew her mother."

"I can't remember specific ages," Kurt told him, "but she wasn't in school yet when they bought the house." He sat back, still staring at the photograph. "Do you have any more of these?"

"A couple." Nicholas handed over two other snapshots, each of them showing Emily, a laughing, happy Emily.

"It's obvious you knew a side of her no one else did," Kurt mused. "I remember her as a cool, rather overbearing snob. Sorry." He shrugged. "I didn't mean to be rude."

"No apology necessary," Nicholas said easily as he rose to his feet. He began pacing the spacious confines of Kurt's office. "Apparently Emily had her own ghosts to contend with. I'm

230

only sorry she wouldn't let me share her life. But now, to learn that I do have a daughter is of far more concern to me than worrying about what might have been if her mother had never run away."

"I suppose you want me to help smooth the way for you to get to know Shay?"

"Will you?"

"Not until I see a hell of a lot more than these three photographs. Shay Michaels is very precious to me, and I won't allow anyone to hurt her."

"Believe me," Nicholas said with quiet dignity, "the last thing I want to do is hurt my daughter. The detective who handled the investigation for me is waiting outside. May I ask him to join us?"

Kurt nodded, his expression grim as he, too, rose to his feet. The two men were of almost identical height, each broad shouldered, each rugged and attractive. For a moment Nicholas regarded the younger man closely, a gentle smile on his face. "Last night, when Ian Deaton pointed out your table, I immediately jumped to the conclusion that you were my son. Had it been so, I would have been proud to acknowledge you."

"Well if Shay does prove to be your daughter, Nicholas, then you just might get me as well," Kurt remarked dryly after instructing Colleen to send in Ian Deaton. "You should be warned that Shay is nothing if not the stubbornest female on this earth. She's had her eye on me since she took her first step, and neither hell nor high water has changed her mind. I'm considering becoming a Trappist monk to escape the yoke of matrimony."

Nicholas chuckled, finding he genuinely liked this Kurt Barron. "I must admit, I don't know whether to wish you good luck or tell you that I hope Shay is successful."

"Well, at least you're trying to remain neutral." Kurt grinned. "That's a good start."

The door opened and Ian Deaton walked in, carrying a much scarred briefcase.

Shay slowly straightened, her hands going to the small of her back and pressing. "I'd give all my worldly wealth for one minute alone with the miserable bastard responsible for this," she muttered as Jane entered the kitchen, carrying a plastic bucket full of ammonia cleaner.

"Your 'worldly wealth' wouldn't buy you a second with the pig." Jane placed several bottles of cleaner in the cupboard above the sink. "Your bathroom is clean again. For the world of me, I can't figure out why he—they—whoever, got the brilliant idea to fingerpaint with your makeup. It was a darned greasy job to clean up."

"This whole apartment was a pain to clean.

By the way, you can stop worrying. The guy just finished putting on the new lock."

"Great," Jane said, relieved. "I could just imagine some madman remembering he had your key and deciding to pay you a little visit one dark night."

"Thanks, sister dearest. I really needed that. You make me wish I'd gotten up at the crack of dawn this morning and left with Becky, the lucky dog."

"I don't know how lucky Becky is, having to do all that traveling. But it was very sweet of Kurt to take the two of you in last night," Jane said kindly. "I hope you didn't try to insult him while you were there."

"Oh, I was very nice to him," Shay assured her without looking up from where she was wiping down the bottom cupboards. "As a matter of fact, all three of us went to bed almost as soon as we got to Kurt's house." Which was no lie, Shay thought fleetingly. However, she decided not to add that she and Kurt had made love and talked till the first tinges of daybreak were marking the sky.

"That's good. I'm sure you needed your rest after such an awful experience," Jane consoled her.

"Hmmmm. At least," Shay murmured.

"I do wish you'd change your mind and stay with us till the house is ready. It bothers me, you being alone here."

"You're sweet to ask me, and I appreciate it. But I feel some responsibility to Becky. After all, she does live with me, and some of her things were damaged in the fire. She doesn't have any other place to go."

"Oh, I suppose you're right, but I'll worry all the same. And I'm sure Kurt won't be happy with the idea."

"Of course he will, once I explain it to him," Shay said confidently. Privately she was preparing herself for a battle royal. Kurt was going to hit the ceiling, and she darn well knew it.

"I have to go, honey. Susie's probably just waking up about now, and I want to be sure her temperature is still normal. This cold has made her feel so terrible."

"You shouldn't have gotten a sitter. You could have brought her with you."

"Oh, really?" Jane quipped. "It's plain you haven't the faintest idea what a three-year-old can get into." She walked over and dropped a kiss on Shay's cheek. "Give me a call later."

"Will do." Shay saw her to the door, then returned to the task of washing down the cupboards. Once that was done, the apartment would be back to normal. It would never be home to her, but it would suffice till her house was back to normal.

When Jane pulled into the driveway of the attractive native stone house she shared with Ted and Susie, she was surprised to see Ted's red Porsche as well as Kurt's Mercedes. She frowned. Had she forgotten something? Had Ted changed his day off without telling her?

By the time she entered the house and followed the sound of the men's voices to the deck off the family room, she had worked herself into a real tizzy.

"Why didn't you remind me this morning that you were taking the day off?" she demanded of Ted the minute she stepped through the French doors. She walked straight over to where her tall blond husband was seated at the wrought iron table and dropped a kiss on his forehead. She greeted Kurt the same way, then looked politely but inquiringly at Nicholas Pappolas. "Ted darling, you also failed to mention that we were having guests for lunch."

All three men had gotten to their feet upon her arrival, and were regarding her with an assessing gleam in their eyes.

Ted smiled reassuringly. "You aren't cracking up, sweetheart, so don't worry. I hadn't planned on taking today off, and when I left this morning, I had no idea I'd be bringing guests home for lunch." He took her hand, then turned to Nicholas. "Jane, I'd like for you to meet Nicholas Pappolas. Nicholas, this is my wife, Jane."

"Mr. Pappolas," Jane said softly. "How nice to meet you. Are you in Flagstaff on business or for pleasure?" What a handsome gentleman, she was thinking. He seemed so nice.

"Both, and please call me Nicholas."

"All right, Nicholas, and I'm Jane." She looked up at Kurt, who was standing to her left. "What's your excuse for goofing off in the middle of the day? By the way, did you know you were losing your houseguests?"

"What do you mean?" Kurt asked sharply as they each took their seats again.

"I've been with Shay, helping her get the apartment back to normal. She plans on staying there this evening, and every other evening, till the repairs on the house are completed."

"Did you try to get her to move in with us?" Ted inquired.

"I tried everything." Jane shrugged. "Fortunately, we're all perfectly aware of how granitelike my little sister's will is once she's made up her mind to do something." She looked apologetically at Nicholas. "I'm sorry to be discussing family matters this way, Nicholas, but my sister's apartment was broken into last night. It was a tumbled mess this morning, and she's determined to move back in today."

Nicholas shot Kurt an inquiring look, then asked if Shay had been harmed.

"Oh, no," Jane assured him. "She was out with Kurt, but her roommate was hit on the head."

"From what the police can figure out," Kurt spoke up, "it would appear as if the break-in was more a case of someone 'looking' for something to do. One other apartment was about to be entered when the owners returned unexpectedly. Rather, they think it was about to be entered. They say they think they heard someone trying the door. However, the police were unable to find any signs of an attempted forced entry."

"Oh," Jane said quickly, "that's another thing. The locks on Shay's door have been changed."

"Well, at least that's something," Ted remarked. "I still think I'll have a go at trying to get her to stay with us."

"Good luck," his wife said curtly. "Oh, dear, I forgot about Susie. Is she still asleep?"

"No." Ted shook his head. "The sitter took her for a walk. She was free of fever and I thought it would do her good. Okay?"

"Yes. She'll like that."

"Janey." Kurt took that moment to hitch his chair closer to hers. "I know you're wondering why on earth the three of us decided to drop in on you, aren't you?"

"Now that you mention it"—Jane smiled at him—"why are you here? I usually don't entertain three such distinguished men in the middle of the day. Especially in faded jeans and a sweatshirt."

Ted laughed, then ruffled her hair. Jane playfully slapped at his hand, then regarded Kurt sternly. "Ever since I've known you, you've always been the instigator. What's going on?"

Kurt gestured with one hand toward Nicholas, who was steadily watching Jane. "I'm innocent as a babe, Jancy. Nicholas is the culprit."

"In a pig's eye! You only say that because you're jealous. Nicholas is too handsome to be a culprit."

"I hope you feel that way once you've heard me out, Jane," Nicholas told her. He leaned forward, his forearms resting on the edge of the table. "I'm about to tell you a story, Jane. A story that could cause you to hate me, though I hope not. Nothing that was done was meant to harm you or anyone else. We were simply two people who met and fell in love. We both should have realized the hopelessness of the situation, but when love enters a relationship, one's rationale becomes mysterious and complex."

Jane cocked her head at an angle, her gaze puzzled as she studied the man. "You said 'we' were in love, Nicholas. Exactly who are you referring to?"

"Your mother and I."

At the mention of Suzanne, Jane looked stunned. She looked from Ted to Kurt and then back to Nicholas. "Please," she said quietly, "continue. You have my full attention."

Nearly two hours later, as Kurt and Nicholas drove away from the Corley home, Nicholas looked at Kurt. "Do you think she will resent me?"

"Janey? No," Kurt said firmly. "I think you'll find that both Suzanne's daughters are very kind, loving individuals. Shay, for example, goes with me once a month to have dinner with my ninety-two-year-old aunt. Agatha is old and cranky and waspish and insulting. But Shay likes her. Janey, on the other hand, can find something good with the worst derelict. Between you and me, I'd always thought Suzanne adopted them both."

"Well, the test won't really be over until I've told Shay my story, will it?"

"No"—Kurt nodded thoughtfully—"it won't."

"A couple of times today I've thought of hiring her to do the flowers for a banquet or something. But the more I think about it, the more I dislike that idea. I'm fifty-seven years old. At the most I only have twenty—maybe twenty-five—years left. I'm selfish, Kurt. I don't want to waste another minute of the time Shay and I have left."

"Then you've decided to tell her today?"

"Why not? It won't be any less of a shock to her two weeks from now."

"Would you like for me to go with you?"

"I think you'd better. From the way she

239

looked at me last night," Nicholas remarked, laughing, "she would probably call the police if I were to appear at her door today."

"She might at that." Kurt chuckled. "You'd better get ready, her place is just around the corner."

CHAPTER FOURTEEN

Shay let herself out of the apartment and hurried to her car. She started the engine, then began driving. There was no particular destination fixed in her mind. In fact, she thought ridiculously, as she made each turn of the steering wheel by instinct rather than paying scrupulous attention to detail, she felt quite positive her mind had dried up. It must have done so. Otherwise, she asked herself, why hadn't she uttered a single word while Nicholas Pappolas told her his story and afterward?

After he had finished, she'd sat like a zombie for several tense moments, then calmly got up, murmured a barely audible "Excuse me," and left. For an hour and a half—or had it been longer? She shook her head, unable to put a time frame on it—she had sat like a blinking donkey while the most extraordinary story she'd ever heard was repeated. Repeated. Yes, that was what he'd done. He'd *repeated* the story to her after having first gone to Kurt and then Jane. No one could fault the man for not going about a task with extreme caution and attention to detail. That fact alone must have endeared him to Kurt.

She still couldn't believe it.

The tall, distinguished gentleman from the evening before, who had stared at her throughout dinner, had calmly but very kindly informed her that he was her father. That he and her mother, the unbending, seldom happy Suzanne Michaels, had come together in moments of passion. And that from their passion had sprung a child. She, Shay Michaels, was that child. Why hadn't her mother ever told her the truth? Why hadn't she ever told Jane the truth? It simply wasn't fair.

Tears came to her eyes, forcing her to pull the van into a shopping-center parking lot. She leaned her forearms against the steering wheel and simply stared into space. Her mother had told her a lie about one father, and now this Nicholas Pappolas had suddenly appeared in her life with the mind-numbing announcement that he was her father. Was it really the truth?

Of course it was the truth. The poor man had enough documented evidence to have proven his case before the United States Supreme Court. And whether or not she wanted to believe Nicholas Pappolas, what about Kurt?

242

That sobering thought caused Shay momentarily to curb her wildly galloping imagination. Kurt was no fool. If he'd had the slightest doubt regarding the story, he would never have let Nicholas get to Jane or Shay. She knew without even asking that Kurt would have done some checking himself before letting the matter proceed.

Okay, Shay conceded grudgingly, this was probably true. But how was she to handle the proof? Shay asked herself. What was she to do with a father, when she'd spent twenty-three years without one? She already had a very nice family, thank you. She had Jane and Ted and Susie . . . and there was Kurt. In spite of her abject misery she couldn't help but grin at that thought. Poor Kurt was going to be family as well, just as soon as she grew weary of chasing him. He knew it and she knew it. It was only a matter of time before she wore down his defenses and he allowed himself to be caught.

But what about Nicholas Pappolas? Pappolas. She rolled the name around on her tongue. Shay Pappolas. Not bad, she quietly reflected, not bad at all. But she immediately threw up another roadblock. If she were to accept Nicholas as her father, there would also be responsibility on her part. Could she handle that? At the moment she was so wrapped up in Kurt, she wasn't sure she could cope with something as important as learning to adapt to a father she'd met less than three hours ago.

And then there was Jane. Shay slowly shook her head. She couldn't allow Jane to feel as if she were being deserted. Would her sister be able to accept this tall, distinguished Greek millionaire suddenly dropping into their lives?

With a sinking feeling that she must return to her apartment and face whatever it was one faced in such circumstances, Shay started the van and began the return trip. When she parked in her usual spot in the parking lot of the complex, she was rather relieved to see that Kurt hadn't left. That meant Nicholas—er . . . her father—was still there as well. It would have been very embarrassing if they had left.

She squared her shoulders, got a good grip on her emotions, then marched inside.

The minute she opened the door and entered the room, two pairs of eyes turned and stared at her. Shay was tempted to run back out into the hall, but she controlled the urge to do so. "I'm sorry for running out on you like that, but to be honest, your story frightened me." She was looking at Nicholas as she spoke, and was surprised at the compassion she saw in his blue eyes. Blue eyes, the same as hers.

Nicholas got to his feet and met her, his hands reaching for hers. "There's nothing to apologize for, my dear." His grasp was strong but gentle, Shay was thinking. Just like Kurt.

She glanced at Kurt, who was standing back, keenly observing every move. What was he thinking? Wasn't it ironic, Shay was thinking. He'd always "known" he was illegitimate. She'd never even considered that such a label applied to her.

His gaze seemed to be asking her if she was all right. Shay smiled at him. "I'm fine," she answered, then looked at the man who had gone to so much trouble to find her and smiled. "I've been told—on more than one occasion— that I'm mean and nasty-minded; I swear and I'm stubborn as the devil. On the positive side, I like old people, children, and animals. I have a passion for plants and"—she glared at Kurt— "I get very angry when people pour bourbon in them."

"Er . . . I assure you I'll refrain from pouring bourbon into your plants, Shay," Nicholas promised with amusement lurking in his eyes. "As to your other characteristics, let me learn them as I get to know you. What others might see as nasty-minded, I might consider courageous."

"Ohh." Shay beamed at him, then surprised herself and Nicholas by going up on tiptoe and kissing him on the cheek. "I think having you for a father is going to be fantastic."

"You've been warned, Nicholas," Kurt said.

"Don't let her fool you. She's mean as a baby rattler."

Nicholas stood beaming down at his daughter, his grip on her hands showing no sign of slackening. "You'll have to forgive me, Kurt, but I prefer to think of her as being absolutely perfect."

Kurt threw back his head in mock dismay. "Now I know I'm leaving town."

Shay smiled like a contented kitten. "Eat your heart out, Mr. Barron, eat your heart out. Now," she said briskly, "I don't know about the two of you, but I'm starved. This business of being reunited with a father I never knew I had in the first place has given me a tremendous appetite."

"I don't believe it." Kurt looked surprised. "She's actually going to cook lunch for us."

"Not on your life, you great hulking toad," he was abruptly informed. "We're going out to eat. We're also going to call Jane and have her meet us." She looked up at Nicholas, a certain defiance showing in her eyes, eyes so very much like his own. "Janey and I are very close. I hope you'll understand."

"Shay, if you'd ever lived alone, except for servants, in a huge, secluded house, if you'd ever been wealthy and had been able to buy anything your heart desired but were lonely, you'd realize how wonderful it is to know that not only have I found one daughter, but, if she'll let me, I'll take Jane and Susie as well. I didn't come looking for you with the idea of picking and choosing, honey. I knew you and your sister were close before I ever left New York, and I was prepared to accept her as well. You've failed to consider one very important thing. Jane's also Emily's daughter."

"What do you mean, my uncle flew to Arizona yesterday?" Phillip stormed out at Kathryn Bolt, who'd been Nicholas' private secretary for fifteen years.

The attractive brunette stood her ground. "Exactly what I said. In fact, he left shortly after lunch. Will there be anything else, Phillip?"

"With my uncle away, *Miss Bolt,* I think it appropriate that the staff refer to me as Mr. Norcross. After all, I am in charge."

Kathryn said nothing for several seconds, merely staring at him. Finally, she gave a ghost of a nod at the glaring young man. "Very well, if you say so . . . *Mr. Norcross.*" Then she rested her elbows on the desk and stared at him.

Phillip could feel the embarrassing stain of red spreading over his throat and rapidly rushing to his face. Damn the bitch! When he was in charge, Kathryn Bolt would be the first to go. He'd put up with enough humiliation from her for ten men.

"Well?" he said angrily.

"Well . . . ?" Kathryn repeated, a questioning look on her face.

"Why did Uncle Nicholas go to Arizona?"

"Personal business." She smiled coolly. "If there's nothing else I can do for you, Mr. Norcross, please excuse me. I'm taking the next three days off, and I'm anxious to get on my way."

"If that's the case," he snarled, "what made you come into the office this morning?"

"Because Mr. Pappolas asked me to do a favor for him."

"And of course when my uncle says frog, you jump, don't you?"

"Precisely," Kathryn promptly replied. "First of all, Mr. Pappolas is a gentleman. He's courteous to his staff, and he abhors those at various executive levels who think it impressive to throw their weight around." She collected her purse from a drawer, slipped a folder, of which Phillip was trying his darndest to read the label, into a soft leather briefcase, then rose to her feet. "Have a nice day, Mr. Norcross."

Phillip stood rooted to the spot directly in front of her desk and watched her leave the room. He felt for all the world as if he'd just been dismissed—and by a mere secretary at that! He clenched his hands into tight fists, a further affirmation of his rage.

Well . . . he'd show Kathryn Bolt, along with several other undesirables in the company, just who was boss. Not only was he the only intelligent choice to replace Nicholas, he *wanted* it more than any of the others. He was hungry for it.

"Pappolas Shipping." He mouthed the word, the sound of it bringing a certain excitement racing through him, as it always did. Pappolas Shipping was his, he silently declared. Nicholas might have founded it and brought it where it was today, Phillip thought grudgingly, but he was useless now—dead weight. There were new and more innovative ideas to be fed into the corporate structure of the business.

But to do those things, Phillip told himself, he must be in control. And to be in control, he must see that Nicholas's bastard heir was eliminated, that the blackmailer was eliminated, and then . . . He grinned evilly. Wouldn't it be a shame if poor Uncle Nicholas, devastated over the death of his so recently found child, were to kill himself or meet some type of unfortunate accident?

Phillip left Kathryn Bolt's office and made his way to his own domain, ignoring the pleasant greeting of his secretary. He walked over and stared out the window, as the most interesting thoughts began slipping through his mind. Why not have the gentleman with whom he was already doing "business" perform the same service for one Shay Michaels? Later, it would be easy to arrange for Nicholas to commit "suicide" over the death of his only child. Phillip smiled. The circumstances being what they were, no one would doubt for a moment that his uncle's death could be anything *but* suicide.

The more he thought of the idea, the more appealing it became. His hands gripped the edge of the window ledge in almost hysterical anticipation. It wasn't inconceivable that within two to three months he could be at the helm of Pappolas Shipping. He intended to move quickly and decisively. He stood taller, prouder, as the thought of power and wealth pumped his adrenaline to an alarming high. He, Phillip Norcross, finally was to be in a position befitting a man of his ability.

For the next few days after learning that Nicholas Pappolas was her father, Shay found herself racing against the clock in an attempt to take care of her business and spend as much time as possible with him. They had lunch together, they went for drives, and Shay even cooked for him. Jane and Susie and Ted were included as well, and in no time the five of them had begun acting and functioning as a family.

Her father. She smiled. The two words, while certainly important in anyone's life, hadn't the significance in her case, or Jane's, since neither of them could remember the man they'd been told was their father.

And true to his word, Shay thought proudly, Nicholas had accepted Jane and little Susie and Ted into his heart as readily as if his blood flowed in their veins. She was learning something new every day about this newest relative of hers.

A grin of amusement spread over her face as she recalled the confrontation that had taken place when he'd insisted she not stay alone in her apartment. And of course Kurt hadn't helped the situation at all, she remembered.

"The matter is settled," Nicholas had announced in a hard-as-nails voice after listening to Jane trying to persuade Shay to stay at the Corley house for the next few days. Shay, Kurt, and Nicholas had been invited to Jane and Ted's for dinner in celebration of the first week since Shay and Nicholas were united. Everything had gone well till Kurt brought up the question of why Shay hadn't stayed at his house.

"It certainly makes more sense than going back to that damned apartment." He scowled, the furrowing of his wide forehead causing his dark, thick brows to meet in a straight line.

Jane cast Ted and Nicholas a look of comical resignation.

"Do you mind keeping a decent tongue in

your head?" Shay hissed as she took a serving of roast beef onto her plate. "Jane has gone to a lot of trouble to make this an 'enjoyable' occasion." She was happy and finding Nicholas an absolute joy to be with, she told herself. The only thing marring her world was the fact that she was exhausted, and she hadn't had any time to be alone with Kurt. On the other hand, she thought grimly, why the hell should she want to be with the obnoxious ass?

"Are you implying that my presence is hindering Janey's efforts?" Kurt countered.

"I'm sure she doesn't mean anything of the kind, Kurt." Nicholas entered the fray as peacemaker.

"Not at all," Shay said sweetly. "I 'know' you're hindering Janey's efforts!"

"I seriously doubt that, Ms. Michaels," Kurt threw out arrogantly. "Unlike you, your sister has a reasonable, sensible head on her shoulders. If some bastard had broken into her apartment, I seriously doubt she would have gone back the next day and sat waiting for him to return the second time and choke hell out of her."

"Peas, Dad?" Jane smiled benignly at Nicholas, who was observing the dueling couple with interest.

"If Janey is so sensible, then why the hell did she invite you to dinner?"

"Thank you, my dear." Nicholas smiled at

Jane. "I think I will. Peas, Shay?" he offered the dish to his scowling, fire-eating offspring.

"I detest peas. Janey fixed those things for Mr. Barron. He's the pea-eater."

"Personally, Shay, I agree with Kurt," Nicholas interjected. "I really don't care for you being there alone. And now, since your roommate was called to New York earlier than expected, I don't see why you can't move in with Jane or come share my suite with me until your house is available. However, if neither of those suggestions appeals to you, I'll come stay with you."

"That's impossible," Shay said stiffly. "I only took a one-bedroom apartment."

"Nonsense." Nicholas smiled. "You have a sofa, don't you? I can sleep there easily enough."

Shay stared daggers at Kurt, then favored her father with a slightly lesser look. "Greek millionaires can't sleep on sofas. Can we discuss this later?"

"Of course." Nicholas nodded graciously. "I'd like to point out one thing, however. I wasn't always a millionaire, and I'm only half Greek. My mother was an American. In the meantime, why don't we get on with this delicious meal Janey has prepared for us? Afterward, I'm going to spend the afternoon with Susie."

Later, when they were alone, Shay apologized to Jane for her outburst.

"Don't you dare," Jane murmured sympathetically. She wasn't fooled in the least. Shay was under tremendous pressure, and Jane recognized all the signs. Her involvement with Kurt was becoming more frustrating due to the lack of time she could devote to it; Nicholas's arrival, while a happy one for all concerned, had added its own unique pressure. Jane felt helpless. She knew there wasn't a single thing she could do for her sister but be there for her.

"What with Dad's suddenly appearing in our lives, you're on edge. As for you and Kurt's arguing . . ." She lifted her hands dismissively. "That's become so routine, I don't even hear the two of you."

"Getting to know Dad has been a delight, hasn't it?" Shay sighed. She placed the last dirty spoon into the dishwasher, then rinsed off her hands and watched as Jane finished wiping up.

Jane paused in her cleaning and stared into space for a moment. "It really has been. And to be perfectly honest, Shay, I still find the entire story to be incredible. All the facts are bizarre. My father was a man named John Crawford, your father was—is Nicholas Pappolas . . . and mother changed our names to Michaels. Do you suppose it was guilt that made her hide from Nicholas?"

"You mean because of being married while she had the affair and became pregnant?"

"Yes. Remember, that was twenty-three years ago. People weren't nearly as forgiving as they are now."

"Mother was such an unhappy woman," Shay quietly mused. "She lost her husband she obviously loved, months before he actually died, she loved another man, was pregnant by that man, but refused to let him know. Knowing her and how she viewed everything, I can't help but wonder if she wasn't afraid she was being punished when your father died. Now that I know the story, I can better understand that awful sadness I used to see in her eyes."

"What I don't understand, though, is why she didn't let us know any of this as we got older." Jane turned and looked at Shay. "And why, once she was widowed, and after you were born, she didn't get in touch with Dad."

"I don't know. She must have missed Ni—er —Dad terribly."

"It's hard getting used to saying the word, isn't it?" Jane smiled.

"And how. I've even been on the point a couple of times of calling him Mr. Pappolas."

"Well, whatever we call him, Susie is thrilled to death to have her own private Gramps. With only Ted's mother for a grandparent, I think the little tyke felt cheated."

"You know," Shay remarked in a subdued

voice, "I get weepy every time I think of him being so alone since his wife died. What if he hadn't decided to try one more time to find us?"

"We'd have been the losers, wouldn't we?" Jane suggested wisely.

Later, Shay went back over to the greenhouse to do some work. She'd taken on a new customer; one of the state's larger banks was opening a branch in Flagstaff in two days. She'd made daily trips to the location getting the huge planter in the lobby ready, but still needed to include several items in the load of plants and supplies that would be going over tomorrow.

It was quiet in the greenhouse, and a little on the cool side. She walked into a small closetlike enclosure at the rear of the structure and checked the thermostat, making sure the temperature was well within the safe range.

"All I need is for something to go wrong and all my plants to die," she muttered as she backed out of the tiny space, and right into a solid wall of muscle.

Before she could open her mouth to scream, a large hand covered her mouth, and Kurt's voice sounded close to her ear. "What the flaming hell do you mean by working at night, by yourself, and not locking the damned door?"

With each word he spoke, his voice continued to rise. By the time he was finished, he'd swung her around to face him. He was fairly shouting and his eyes were glowing like two darkened embers.

Shay was ready to lash out the minute he stopped to draw a breath. But as she opened her mouth to begin her tirade, she caught a glimpse of something else in those eyes.

Concern.

It suddenly struck her that for all her griping and bitching about how Kurt treated her, very few times had she considered that there was nothing written in stone anywhere in the world that said it was his duty to watch over her. No, she thought in that brief moment of reflection as their gazes met and held, he'd never "had" to do it, but he had. No one asked it of him, no one demanded it of him. He cared, and for Kurt that had been enough.

A slightly trembling hand reached up and touched his sensuous lips, her fingers lightly moving back and forth. "How is it that when I'm most annoyed with you, something snaps in my brain and I find myself remembering all sorts of admirable things you've done for me?" she asked huskily.

"That's nice to hear even if I'm angry with you about the unlocked door," he rasped. "For days now I've been under the distinct impression that you'd forgotten all about me. I don't like being ignored by you, honey."

His hands on her shoulders began slipping

effortlessly over her shoulders and back, dipping down to her buttocks. It was as if he was committing to memory each and every line of her body. One hand ducked between them and grazed the tips of her breasts.

Shay closed her eyes against the tiny tremors of red-hot passion shooting off inside her. She felt herself being enfolded in his strong arms and cradled against his wide, incredibly sexy chest. "You do know that I love you, don't you?" she whispered. The second the words were out of her mouth she wanted to take them back. On the other hand, she reasoned, what did it matter? Kurt didn't think her capable of feeling something as lasting as deep love for a man.

"You know something, sweetheart, I'm beginning to think you really do," he surprised her by saying.

Shay jerked back as far as his arms would allow and stared disbelievingly at him. "Say that again . . . please?" There was such incredible excitement in her eyes that Kurt smiled.

"I believe you. Why are you grinning like a Cheshire cat?" he demanded, though his tone of voice was belied by his crushing her to him and almost breaking her ribs.

"Ouch!" she complained, immediately feeling his hold loosen. "Shame on you," she teased. "I'm smaller than you. As for your question . . ." She sighed. "It's the first positive sign you've shown toward acknowledging that I'm a woman."

"Er . . . exactly what do you call it when I make love to you?" Kurt asked indignantly.

Shay laughed. "Weeell. I suppose you have a point. But you must admit you've tried to rain on my parade at every turn."

"Oh—I admit it, all right. But I think you would have done the same thing. All I wanted was assurance that you knew what you wanted. Even Janey has had her doubts."

"My sister has doubts about everything," Shay told him. "I love her dearly, but at times she is the eternal pessimist."

"By the way, Shay Michaels—I mean . . . Pappolas. I love you too," he added huskily.

"I know." The faintest glimmer of tears rushed to her eyes. "I feel guilty," she said quietly.

Kurt frowned. What the hell was she talking about. "Why?" he asked cautiously.

"Because I'm so happy. You love me, and I have a father. Even to an old cynic like you, that has to be something."

After dropping a quick kiss on her trembling lips, Kurt pulled a stool forward with the toe of his shoe, then sat down and pulled Shay between his jean-clad thighs. "Before you rush out and kidnap a minister, sweetheart, I want you to think about waiting a few months."

Shay frowned. "Minister? Wait a few months?" she repeated in a whispery voice. "Kurt, are you by any chance proposing . . . in a *very* roundabout way, of course?"

"I am," he said sternly. "I've decided to stop running and let you catch me."

"Decent of you. And when did you arrive at this momentous decision?"

"Damned if I know," Kurt offered defeatedly. "Forever, I guess."

"You're a quick learner, Mr. Barron."

"What about waiting? Are you going to cooperate?" he asked shrewdly as he felt the soft touch of her fingers slip through the opening of his shirt and begin whispering softly against his chest.

"Sure, Kurt," she whispered against his lips, her fingers finding the masculine nipples hidden in his thick, curly hair. She felt them harden beneath her touch and smiled. "Whatever you say."

"That'll be the day." Kurt sucked in a rush of air as if he'd been kicked by a mule. "Spend the night with me, Shay."

"Since you asked so nicely, Mr. Barron, I'd be delighted to."

Kurt rose to his feet, then began striding toward the door, half carrying, half pushing Shay along with him. As he waited for her to lock up, his dark eyes narrowed. "You think I forgot about you being in there without locking the door, don't you?"

"Now, why on earth would I do such a foolish thing as that?" Shay asked as she looked up at him, knowing from his expression that regardless of the fact that within a very short time she would be writhing in his arms in a world of painfully exquisite ecstasy, she was about to receive a lecture. "You have the memory of an elephant, and are blessed with the stubbornness of a jackass!"

CHAPTER FIFTEEN

Shay hummed as she drove along, marveling at how beautifully the Mercedes handled. Kurt had been correct early that morning when he'd told her that she would like it.

"But what if I scratch or dent it?" she'd wailed, looking longingly at the car but reluctant to trust her driving. Her darn van was on the fritz and she was carless at a time when she was unable to stop long enough even to take a deep breath.

"It's a car, Shay," Kurt had patiently spoken, his large hand smoothing the lines of worry from her forehead. "Personally, I don't give a damn if you scrape it in ten different places, as long as you don't get hurt. Okay?"

Shay threw him an uneasy look, then began sidling up to the car as if fearful of its screaming in protest and running down the street at the sight of her. "The last time I borrowed Jane's car, I backed into a concrete post. I also dented a fender on one of your other vehicles. When I

rented the car while my van was being re-
paired after my most recent accident, I broke a
headlight and damaged the grill." The low-
voiced litany was being offered all during the
time Kurt was getting her inside and urging
her with gruff reassurance to insert the key
into the ignition and start the engine.

He looked down at her, amusement rampant
in his rough-hewn features. "Take care, sun-
shine," he teased, then kissed her hard.

For once the touch of his lips failed to sway
the dark cloud of misery hanging over her
head. She was convinced she was going to do
something terrible to his darn car. Kurt was
still laughing at her when she backed from the
driveway and turned down the street.

Now, several hours later, Shay was confident
of her driving, and knew she would regret having to return the Mercedes to Kurt.

As her thoughts flitted from her dad and the
business trip he was on, to Kurt and her cam-
paign to wear down his stubbornness against
setting a date for their marriage, Shay idly
glanced in the rearview mirror. Funny . . .
She frowned. The same dark-green sedan she'd
noticed several times already, was still behind
her. She slowed to ten miles an hour below the
speed limit for city traffic, but the car made no
effort to pass her.

Strange, she thought.

After the next two stops to check the plants

263

in an advertising firm, and a quick swing by the grocery store, Shay saw that she had lost her tail. Her imagination had been having a field day, she thought, grinning.

She drew a sigh of relief. "Thank goodness." And with a few minutes spare time on her hands, she decided to drop in on Kurt. She cast a critical eye over the light-blue skirt and blouse she was wearing.

As always, Colleen Gray was dressed to perfection. Not a hair was out of place, and she looked as if her makeup had been permanently applied to her face. Don't be catty, Shay's conscience scolded.

"I hear congratulations are in order," Colleen cooed the minute she saw Shay. "I know it will be a fantastic marriage. How could it be otherwise? Kurt is such a wonderful person."

Shay was tempted to empty the vase of yellow flowers sitting on the desk over Colleen's head. Instead, she smiled coolly and asked if Kurt was busy.

The annoying woman buzzed her boss, then waved Shay through with some gutsy remark.

"I do not like that woman," Shay announced the minute the door was closed behind her.

Kurt got up from his desk grinning. He walked around the end and met her halfway. "I'm not especially fond of her, but she is one hell of a secretary." He took her into his arms and kissed her till Shay didn't wonder if her knees would support her, she *knew* they wouldn't. She smiled dazedly at him and hung on for dear life.

"You get a special kick out of doing that, don't you?"

"What crime am I being accused of now?" he teased as he dropped down into a chair, then pulled her onto his lap. "What do I get a special kick out of doing to you?" he whispered, his tongue teasing the whorl of her ear and nibbling at the excited pulse at the side of her neck.

"Kissing me—till I—can't stand, teasing me till I'm—ready to scream," she whispered back in tiny half-gasps and starts. "I came by to tell you something very important, and now you've made me forget it."

"What could possibly be more important than sitting on my lap while I kiss you?" he asked seductively.

"I can only think of one thing." Shay grinned impishly.

"Brazen hussy!"

"Mmmmm." She smiled unrepentantly. "Complaining, Mr. Barron?"

"Not in the least, Ms. Michaels. By the way, do you plan on changing your name to Pappolas?"

"I've talked to Dad about it, and we decided not to. Considering who he is, it would only bring a huge amount of publicity that I don't think Janey or I are ready to cope with."

"Very sensible." Kurt nodded. "Besides, your name will be changed in a few months anyway."

"Really? Who knows, I just may be out of the mood by then. You've put up such a dedicated struggle, I find I'm beginning to tire of the chase," she haughtily informed him.

"Then I'd suggest you become rejuvenated, my dear, because you are definitely going to marry me."

"Ahhh," Shay gleefully joined into the argument by saying, "but how can I be sure it's me you really want, Kurt? After all, Nicholas is far wealthier than you. Is it me or the money you know I'll be coming into that's suddenly made you change your mind?"

"Your money, of course," he teased her. "I'm psychic, I knew Nicholas was your father all along and was only waiting for the day he would appear to claim you. Don't you admire my psychic capabilities?"

"Oh, yes." Shay nodded smugly. "But it's the physical ones I'm more enamored with. Especially the ones that control the way you make love to me." She deliberately moved her hips against his thighs, watching the affect of her teasing through narrowed lids.

"My, my," he breathed roughly. "Aren't we brave today." He crushed her to him, his mouth taking hers in a conquest that left little doubt who was master of the situation. When he drew back, a gleam of triumph showed in his eyes as he saw the way her lips were still parted and slightly swollen. There was the faintest pink in her cheeks, and her blue eyes looked as if she'd just awakened. "You look as if you'd just been made love to."

Shay started to tell him that she had been, when she suddenly remembered what it was she wanted to tell him. "I think I was followed today. That's what you made me forget a while ago. Some man in a dark-green sedan trailed me practically all morning. But this afternoon, he seemed to have disappeared."

"The poor devil probably became bored watching you fret and worry over the plants you've got stashed all over town." Kurt tweaked her small nose to mask his concern; secretly, he was beginning to wonder if all the things that had happened to Shay lately had been mere coincidence or if they had been deliberate.

He looked at the facts. He knew—because he'd insisted she do it—that the wiring in her house had been replaced only two years ago. He saw to it personally that her van was serviced once a month, for the simple reason that if left to her own devices, Shay would never think to have the oil checked or anything else. There'd also been the break-in of the apartment and now she thought she was being followed. Scatterbrained at times she may be, he thought worriedly, but she was never an alarmist.

"If it happens again, honey, let me know. Word's bound to get out that you're Nicholas's daughter. And"—he shrugged—"I'm not exactly a pauper, so as the news of our pending marriage begins to circulate, you may become the target of some unwelcome attention."

Kurt dropped a kiss on her cheek, then set her on her feet. He pulled her to him in a move that had her breast on level with his mouth. His lips nibbled at the burgeoning tips, and in seconds the pebbled hardness of her nipples was impudently straining against the thinness of her bra and dress. "But I do hope my attentions are welcome," he rasped huskily.

With more willpower than she'd ever thought herself capable of, Shay suddenly extracted herself from his arms. She put several safe steps between them and smiled at him. "I have three other appointments, Kurt Barron. If I stay here another minute, we'll embarrass ourselves by making use of one of those shamefully comfortable sofas in that other room."

"Shay darling." Kurt grinned lazily at her. "You know me so well."

"I've devoted a lifetime of study to the subject." She threw up one hand. "See you this evening."

"Seven sharp," he reminded her, still sitting and watching her. "And if your friend reappears, give me a call immediately."

"Are you worried that it really could be something?"

"I doubt it is." Then he smiled. "I'm merely protecting all that money you're going to inherit from old Nicholas."

"Toad!" she declared scathingly just as she exited the office. Colleen Gray looked up, startled at such an unfair description of her boss. One look at Shay's face, however, was enough to keep the secretary from commenting. Shay held her composure till she was outside, then she burst into gales of laughter.

John Hunter reached for his drink, one ear carefully trained to the conversation taking place between the two men seated next to him at the bar.

"Can you imagine that?" one of them asked the other.

"Sounds like the old TV show called *The Millionaire*. Remember that? The guy would go up to a house and hand over a check to some unsuspecting Joe for a cool million. I always wondered what it would be like to have that happen."

"Well, that Michaels dame won't have to wonder, pal," man number one remarked. "She not only gets the check, she gets the damn bank it's drawn on. Pappolas Shipping is as solid as Fort Knox."

The talk continued, but John Hunter reached into his pocket and withdrew some bills. He dropped several on the bar, then slipped off the stool and faded into the dimness. All the way back to the motel on the edge of town, he kept reviewing what he'd heard, and trying to fit it in with what he knew about Phillip Norcross.

Phillip Norcross was Nicholas Pappolas's nephew—that was common knowledge. During one of his conversations with Phillip the word *blackmail* had cropped up. Hunter remembered commenting on it, hoping to find out more, but Phillip had refused to offer any further explanation.

He glanced at his watch. It was still early. The best way to get to the root of a puzzle was to go to the best source of information, Hunter decided, and Phillip Norcross was just that. If he had enough reason to want to eliminate the person blackmailing him, then Hunter was almost willing to bet there was some connection between Shay Michaels, Nicholas Pappolas, and Phillip Norcross . . . other than the same blood in their veins. If he could find out for sure, there might be more money in this deal than he had ever expected. . . .

He dialed the New York number, coming straight to the point as soon as Phillip was on the line. "I'm hearing some strange rumors out here that are making me very curious, Norcross," he began immediately, taking advantage by putting Phillip on the defensive.

"I—I don't understand," Phillip began nervously. "Besides, I can't talk right now, I'm in my uncle's office."

"What the hell difference does that make? And speaking of your uncle, why didn't you come out with your uncle to meet your new cousin?" he asked. "And why did I get another telephone call from you and an additional payment by way of Western Union this morning to insure that Miss Michaels encounters the same nasty accident as the blackmailer? Weren't the car accident, the fire, and the burglary attempt I rigged up for you enough? What's the setup, Norcross?"

"That's no concern of yours," Phillip snapped. "You got your money, now do the jobs you were hired for."

"Listen to me, you spineless ass." Hunter's voice came over the wire like the thin, cutting edge of steel. "You don't honestly think I'll be fobbed off with an answer like that, do you? Nicholas Pappolas is money, you damned fool. More money than this piddling amount you've given me to get rid of two people. I'm greedy, Norcross. I want a chance at the mother lode."

"There'll be no mother lode if my uncle gets wind of our transactions," Phillip said quickly,

271

the panic in his voice making it shrill. "I'll get you more money, if that's what you want. It'll take time, though."

"It's becoming clearer and clearer why you want Shay Michaels out of the way, Norcross. She stands between you and Pappolas Shipping. Right?"

"This is too delicate to discuss on the phone."

"Bullshit! Answer me."

"Yes," Phillip yelped like a dog whose paw had been trampled.

"And what's the blackmailer's game? And it better be the truth. 'Cause remember one thing, Norcross, I'll be the last one to see each of these two alive. If what they tell me doesn't correspond with your story, I'll take delight in stripping you of your skin, inch by lousy inch."

"This—this person contacted me a number of months ago with enough information pointing to the fact that my uncle had an heir, that I hired a private detective. Everything I'd been told was confirmed by the PI. But instead of being content with a sum we'd agreed upon, this person decided to become greedy."

"Like me, eh?" Hunter laughed, the sound causing Phillip to tremble.

"I simply can't have that person hounding me for the rest of my life."

"*We* certainly can't, can we?"

Phillip fell back in his chair, perspiration breaking out over his entire body. What had he gotten himself into? Either way he turned he was caught. "No," he murmured dully, "we really can't have it."

There was a spring in Becky Walters's step as she walked toward the front of the apartment complex. She had four whole days off—four whole days in which to finish her business in Flagstaff and complete her packing without having to rush herself to death.

She started to reach for her key, then happened to glance at her watch. Three forty-five. That meant Shay wouldn't be home for at least another hour. Oh, well. She shrugged. She'd just go on in and put on a pot of coffee.

One hand slipped inside the huge shoulder bag and began groping for a large brass key ring with several keys attached. Just as her hand closed around the familiar circle of metal, she felt the distinct presence of another person behind her. So close, she felt the person's breath fanning the back of her neck. A smile touched Becky's face.

"I know you weren't expecting . . ." the words tumbling from her lips became fainter and fainter as she turned, dwindling to a whisper . . . then nothing. For it wasn't Shay standing behind her, but a stranger. A man.

A man approximately five feet ten inches tall, with very thin brown hair and a sallow, unhealthy-looking complexion. He wore dark glasses, but somehow Becky knew that his eyes would be like bottomless black holes . . . no emotion, nothing.

"A-are you looking for anyone in particular?" she finally managed. It was impossible for her to step back from him because the door was almost touching her back and hips. Couldn't he see that he was frightening her? "Will you please move back?"

"I don't want to move back, Becky."

"How do you know my name?" she asked, startled. "Who are you?"

"Why, Becky"—he grinned, and it reminded Becky of pictures she'd seen of cadavers—"are you afraid of me?"

Becky looked up and down the wide corridor in hopes of catching a glimpse of someone. Unfortunately, there was nothing but emptiness and silence—except for the evil man standing in front of her. "What do you want?" she asked again, hysteria beginning to creep into her voice.

"Why don't we talk inside?" he suggested in a cold, harsh tone when the sound of voices could be heard coming their way. "Now," he said menacingly, and caught Becky by her upper arm in a cruel grip. "Open the door."

With hands that could barely hold the key, she did as she was instructed. Perhaps inside she could manage to distract him and get away. But whatever hopes she had in that direction were soon dashed when she was pushed down on the sofa.

"When did you decide to come back to Flagstaff?" he surprised her by asking. How on earth did this awful person know her schedule?

"I've lived here for the last seven or eight months."

"But you've recently been transferred to New York, so don't play games with me. No later than Sunday you left here telling everyone that there'd been some mixup and you were to report to the New York office immediately. Why the lie?"

Becky was so frightened she was practically incapable of speech. Who was this man, and why did he keep asking her such personal questions? "I have four days off, and wanted to spend it here."

He laughed mockingly. "I think you came back here to eliminate your friend Shay." He leaned down suddenly and caught her chin in a hard biting grip. "Let's stop kidding ourselves. Phillip Norcross sends his regards, Miss Walters."

Becky's eyes became glazed with fright. Her heart was pumping at an unbelievable rate of speed, and each breath she drew into her lungs was like a knife cutting deeply and painfully.

"I don't know what you're talking about. I would never harm Shay, and I don't know anyone by that name of Phillip."

"Oh, you know him, all right. You're black-mailing him." He grinned scornfully. "And he hired me to see that you are disposed of."

"Oh, my God!" she exclaimed, scrambling terrified about till she was kneeling on the sofa, clutching at his arms with both hands. "You're the one that set fire to the house and hit me over the head, aren't you? Please," she begged, when he nodded, confirming her suspicions, "let me explain, Mr. . . . ?"

"That would be a unique twist," he sneered. "Why not? But do hurry, won't you? I'm not strong on patience. You can also forget about my name. I seriously doubt we'll be running into each again." He pushed her hands off his arm as if removing an insect, then dropped into one of the chairs facing the sofa, one hand buried in a jacket side pocket.

Becky felt fear rising in her throat like a huge, immovable wedge. Was he fondling a knife . . . a gun? "I only did it for the money," she cried. "Haven't you ever wanted money?"

"You're doing the explaining," he said in an emotionless voice.

"Yes." She nodded, then licked her bone-dry lips. "When I found all those letters Suzanne Crawford—she later changed her name to Michaels—had written to my mother, I realized a gold mine had dropped into my lap. Suzanne kept my mother informed of everything, from the day she left Nevada till a few months before she died. She was the coolest dame I've ever heard of. Do you know she kept a post office box all those years? Her daughters never suspected . . . at least she told my mother they didn't. When she would get a letter from Mom, she would read it, then burn it."

"But your mother kept everything, didn't she?"

"Yes." Becky nodded jerkily. "I knew everything about Shay from the day she was born. All her childhood diseases, her birthmark, likes, dislikes, when she had her first date, learned to drive—"

"Enough," the man held up his hand. "I'm really not that interested."

"Oh." Becky whimpered. She pressed the back of one hand to her mouth, tears moving freely down her cheeks. "Please," she begged, "please. I'll do anything. Just let me live."

"I wonder if Shay Michaels would want to let you live once she knows that you deliberately singled her out, became her roommate and pretended to be her good friend, while all along you and Phillip were plotting her downfall."

"But you don't understand," she cried beseechingly. "She didn't know she was Nicholas Pappolas's daughter. If Phillip had listened to me, she would never have known. With the information I had, I could have become the long-lost daughter Nicholas had never known.

At first Phillip pretended to like that idea, that's the reason I moved in with Shay. It was an opportunity to get to know her more intimately . . . to become more comfortable when I'd eventually replace her."

"Did it ever occur to you that at some point you might have to dispose of Shay Michaels?" he asked flatly.

Becky simply stared at him, unable to think of a reply.

"And you want me to be merciful to you, Miss Walters?"

"My real name is Connors—Becky Connors. I assumed the name of Walters in the event Shay or Jane knew of the close relationship between our mothers."

There was a tense moment of silence. Becky never took her eyes off that cold, expressionless face. What was he thinking? Did he believe her? Would he let her go?

"Why don't we take a little drive?" he pushed himself to the edge of the chair, then stood. "I still have some unfinished business with Miss Michaels."

"No!" Becky cried, pressing harder and harder against the back of the sofa. "Oh, please . . . no!"

A cold, mirthless laugh mingled with her cries for mercy. "Begging excites me." He smiled. "If you beg long enough, I might

change my mind . . . for a little while. Now,"
he said sharply, reaching down and locking his
fingers around her wrists, then jerking her to
her feet, "let's move."

CHAPTER SIXTEEN

"Stay right where you are, Hunter!"

The sharp command paralyzed the man holding Becky's arm so painfully.

"Raise your hands over your head and don't even blink an eyelash," he was told in clipped tones.

Slowly, and with an incredible sense of relief, Becky turned to face the one responsible with saving her life. But instead of one lone man, she saw a veritable army of officers, from plainclothes to uniforms, pistols drawn and ready to fire. They'd been hiding in the bedroom and had heard every word.

In that brief second in time her gaze drifted to a grim-featured Kurt Barron and an equally shaken Nicholas Pappolas. She'd never met the Greek, but she recognized him from his pictures.

A subdued flurry of activity suddenly began to occur as the officers moved cautiously toward John Hunter. One of the uniformed officers pulled her to one side of the room and told her to stay put. Becky didn't argue; she was too relieved to do anything but sit.

Suddenly there was movement behind Kurt, a flash of yellow and white. The movement became Shay. She stepped out from behind the human barricade protecting her, her expression, when she looked at Becky, a mingling of pity and contempt.

Becky rose to her feet and took a determined step toward her, then paused. "I'm only sorry I failed," she hissed.

Shay's gaze narrowed against the hatred she heard in those words. She was still shaken by what she had just witnessed. She would have never guessed that Becky—her good friend—had been behind such an evil scheme. "How sad," she remarked in an emotionless voice.

The real Becky was really becoming evident now. "It's a pity," she said callously. "I'm much more suited to being the daughter of a wealthy man than you."

"How fortunate for me that human beings can't be replaced like clones," Shay replied levelly.

Becky shrugged indifferently, and stared hard at Nicholas. "Only two minor details kept my plans from becoming a reality."

"What were they?" he asked.

"You becoming maudlin in your old age, and that stupid ass Phillip losing his nerve."

"You win some, you lose some," Nicholas murmured. "Thank God I was able to alert the authorities before you or Hunter could harm Shay." He slipped an arm around Shay and pulled her to him. He was only glad that his assistant, Kathryn Bolt, had happened to overhear Phillip's phone conversation with Hunter and alerted him right away. He owed Shay's life to her.

He looked down grimly at Shay. Because of who he was, she'd almost been killed. "I'm so sorry," he whispered against her hair.

She eased back and looked up at him, her heart filled with sympathy for him. "Please, Dad," she said gently, and saw his features relax slightly as she began to talk. "You can't help being who you are, no more than I or anyone else can. I love you, and I'm proud to tell the world that I'm your daughter." She glanced at a sneering Becky, then back to Nicholas. "There'll always be a certain element in society who think the world owes them something. It's unfortunate, but true."

"How did you get so smart?" Nicholas murmured. He dropped a kiss on her forehead, then squeezed her shoulder before releasing her.

"I'm your daughter, of course," she reminded him in a lighthearted attempt at taking his mind off what was happening a few feet from him, and hoping to eliminate any guilt he might be feeling.

"I'm proud of you, Shay Michaels, and I love you with all my heart," she heard Kurt whisper next to her ear. His arms encircled her, and Shay felt incredibly sheltered as she stood between the two tall men.

She looked up at him and smiled. "I know, Kurt. You always have."

Shay walked from the bathroom into Kurt's bedroom, a towel wrapped around her body and another one wrapped turban style around her head.

"You look weird," Kurt teased her. He was standing just inside the room, dressed in nothing but a pair of jeans, and holding a tray loaded with a plate of sandwiches and steaming cups of coffee.

"I won't even box your ears for that remark," she announced blithely. "You may put the food over here on this table, then leave."

"Leave?" he said disbelievingly. He walked over to the table where she'd cleared off some books, and set down the tray. "Why on earth should I leave?"

"Because I'm hungry as a wolf, and I don't think there's enough food for both of us." She laughed.

He reached for her, holding her close . . . nothing more. They'd made love twice within the last hour and a half, and now Kurt wanted nothing more than just to touch her, to hold her in his arms. She was safe, and he wasn't going to let her out of his sight till they were married.

"Has it occurred to you that people, even possibly members of our family, are wondering if we *have* to get married?" she remarked dryly, her fingers curling in and out of the hair on his chest.

Shay felt him shaking. She looked up at him, question in her eyes. "What's so funny?"

"The only one other than Janey with nerve enough to mention it was Agatha." He chuckled.

"She didn't."

"Not two seconds after I arrived at her house to let her know our plans."

"Oh, well." Shay grinned. "I doubt she'd be too upset if it were true. She's been trying to get us together ever since that other Michaels girl threw you over."

They fell silent for a moment, lost in their thoughts of the last twenty-four hours. Shay still shivered each time she thought of that awful man John Hunter whom Phillip had hired to kill herself and Becky. As for Phillip, she tried to be generous and lean toward the idea that his mind had snapped. It must have, she told herself, for him to have committed suicide. His betrayal and his death had left its scars on her father.

"Don't let it spoil this time for us, honey," Kurt broke into the painful reverie. "Your father is fine. It'll take a while for him to forget, but with you and Janey and little Susie helping him, it won't take long. There's someone else who would just love the chance to make his life a little easier."

"Oh? Who?"

"Kathryn Bolt."

"Really?" Shay smiled. "She's a lovely person, isn't she? I'll always think kindly of that dear lady for alerting us to what Phillip had planned for me. As for her and Dad, why not?"

"You wouldn't mind?" Kurt asked. He pulled two chairs up to the table, then motioned for Shay to sit.

"Of course not." She frowned. "What kind of person do you think I am? I don't ever want him to be lonely again. It breaks my heart when I think how he was so alone."

"Well, you can stop worrying now, he will have you around to put up with till he dies," Kurt teased.

"That was unkind," she haughtily informed him, "and I'll get even later. But at the moment I'm going to feed my face." She paused. "There is one thing still bothering me."

"What's that?"

"With John Hunter being wanted by the po-

285

lice in four different states, it's a foregone conclusion that he will spend the rest of his life in prison. What will happen to Becky?"

Kurt was honest. "Prison. There's no way she can possibly avoid it, honey. Becky is one of those cold, calculating types who can hurt people without the slightest qualm. You saw that yourself."

"All I can say is, she had me totally fooled."

They ate in silence, tired but relieved in a way that only comes on the heels of a near tragedy.

Later, when they were back in bed and the room was in darkness, Kurt held her in his arms. "Go to sleep," he whispered. "It's only a few hours till we fly to Vegas."

"Mmmm, I know," she murmured as she snuggled closer. "I think I'm going to be very happy married to you, Mr. Barron."

"The feeling is mutual, Ms. Michaels."

"Can you imagine what it's been like for poor Jane, having to cope with Agatha till we get there?"

"Mmmm. Your father will probably push Agatha out of the plane coming back. The first thing she did when I introduced her to him was to tell him he ought to take a stick to that shameless daughter of his."

Shay took exception to the remark. "That old biddy. I thought she liked me."

"She does." Kurt laughed. "She was talking

about Jane. Nicholas and she were in a hot battle by the time they left for the airport. Of course, she was properly impressed with James, your father's chauffeur."

"So was I. I simply cannot be carted around by someone in uniform like a sack of potatoes. Promise me you will never hire a chauffeur or a butler. If we can't drive ourselves and answer our own door, then we're in terrible shape."

Kurt solemnly promised, shaking with laughter the entire time. She was wonderful, and he was going to spend the rest of his life loving her and caring for her.

"Though tomorrow will officially be the day you become mine," he began huskily, "I know, and you know, that it all began a very long time ago, don't we, kitten?"

"We do indeed, sweetheart, we do indeed. Er . . . Kurt, I've been meaning to talk with you about something."

"Whatever you want, dear heart."

"Wonderful. I need two more new greenhouses. Your backyard is so nice and deep, it would be an excellent place, don't you think?"

"I sure as hell do not," he roared like a wounded bull. "Now, Shay, sweetheart, I don't want any of those damned ugly things littering up my view."

"But, Kurt dearest," she returned with steely undertones, "I thought you said whatever I wanted."

"I did . . . but—"

"Oh, well," disappointment sounding in her voice. "If you really didn't mean it."

"All right! One damned greenhouse. Okay?"

"Of course, dear." Shay smiled. One was more than adequate for the moment. In a few months she would get the other one. It was always such fun reaching a compromise with Kurt.